Forbidden Fruit:
The Preacher's Son

Jasinda Wilder

This is a work of fiction. Names, characters, businesses, places, events and incidents are either the products of the author's imagination or used in a fictitious manner. Any resemblance to actual persons, living or dead, or actual events is purely coincidental.

FORBIDDEN FRUIT: THE PREACHER'S SON

Copyright © 2014 by Jasinda Wilder

ISBN: 978-1-941098-16-5

Cover art by Sarah Hansen of Okay Creations. Cover art copyright © 2014 Sarah Hansen.

Interior book design by Indie Author Services.

One

He was everything I'd never had before. Not just physically, but who he was, inside and out. He was young, strong, kind...and oh my lord, so innocent.

I met him in church. He was sitting near the back, staring out the window and not really paying attention. He was the first person I saw when I walked in those chipped white doors with their faded brass handles. He was coiled into the pew, his knees drawn up, his back hunched, long fingers tapping his broad thighs. His messy black hair swept across his brow, covering one chocolate-brown eye before he brushed it away absently with a thumb. I barely managed to avoid stumbling on a rip in the threadbare carpet when my heel caught. I was so busy taking in the absurd beauty of him that I just about fell flat on my face.

He saw me, then, too, and I think the awe in his eyes is what did it for me. He looked at me like he'd never seen a woman before, he looked at me like a man in a desert looks at a wellspring. I'd never had anyone look at me like that, with a naked desire, unadorned wonder.

The only open seat was at the aisle-end, one row up from him. I took it and sat down just as the white-haired old lady left off her godawful pounding on the poor little tan upright piano. She'd been murdering "Old Rugged Cross" as the congregation took their places, and I was the last one in. Apropos, that was. It was at least ten years since I'd last been in a church—outside of weddings and Christmas—so coming into this little Reformed Baptist chapel was an act of will, a challenge to myself.

I'd fled back to the South after things with Dan went to hell, packed a couple bags, withdrew all the money in my hidden account and hopped the first plane away from nasty old Atlantic City. I wanted distance, I wanted space, I wanted away. I got off the plane in Atlanta, rented a car and drove West until I hit Jackson, Mississippi, and I spent the night there in a seedy old motel off the freeway, roach-infested, stinking to high-heaven, and oh my lord, so quiet.

I grew up in the South, a couple of lifetimes ago. Dan had swept me away from Savannah when I was sixteen, lured me north with promises of money and excitement and fun and endless sex, and he'd provided all that for a few years, and then things changed, as things do with men like him. He got bored, I guess. I wasn't exciting anymore, wasn't new and shiny and tempting. All I can do is guess though, 'cause Dan never told me anything. Just flung money at me and left me for his call girls and his whores and his gambling bunnies and who knows what else. I doubt he ever noticed I was gone, probably. He didn't care what I did, and he was so rich from owning the casino that I could siphon off money left and right and he never said a word. I started that about two years in, when I realized he didn't really love me. It took a long time, but eventually I had enough money stashed away that I knew I could make it on my own, and I split.

By then, of course, he never bothered with me. Rarely came home, never spoke to me. I was just the trophy wife, beautiful and pointless. I tried to find satisfaction elsewhere, once, with one of the card dealers, but Dan made it violently clear, to me and to the poor dealer, that he wouldn't stand for it. I never tried that again.

So, I ran off with a couple million dollars and no clue what to do with myself.

I buzzed north from Jackson in my little Audi TT, top down, feeling finally free. I'd spent a while in Jackson, maybe a year, a year and a half, just taking time to be me. Then, one day, I up and took a little drive, followed US-49 into this tiny little place in the middle of nowhere, full of nothing. It was slow and sleepy and beautiful in its own way, and I liked it, found an empty house to rent, filled it with new things, moved in, and that was how I ended up in little Yazoo City.

The thing to remember about the South is that in little places like Yazoo, you go to church. You just do. You don't have to believe it, but you pay your dues and pretend like everyone else.

I picked that church because it was a cute little building, white clapboards and three cracked concrete steps and a steeple with a black iron bell. There was a cemetery out back behind it, full of ancient headstones from the civil war and before, surrounded by a tall wrought-iron fence. Farther back still was a little knoll crowned by a spreading oak tree, complete with a rope swing. I pictured myself on the swing, just kicking my heels in the humid air and that was it...that was the church I'd go to.

Oh my lord, how little did I know what that decision would start.

Sitting there listening to the pastor's booming, stentorian voice, I felt the dark-haired young man watching me, trying gamely not to stare and failing. I liked his eyes on me. I felt sexy sitting there with his dark eyes straining for a glimpse of my breasts.

He looked about twenty-one or twenty-two, and he had the tan skin and lean muscle of a man who spends all his time outside, working hard and playing hard. He had a thin white scar along his jaw, and I wondered how he'd gotten it. His hands were toying with the crease in his khaki pants, and I wanted so badly to feel those hands on me. That wanting him to touch me, it was a sudden desire, springing up in my belly and taking hold. It was silly, because I was turning thirty-four in a few weeks and I'd just gotten shut of a man, yet here I was wanting this sexy beast of a guy just out of his teens.

I was twisted in the pew, sitting sideways with my legs crossed, a casual enough position, but one carefully thought-out to let me look at him, and to give him a good eyeful of my thighs and my breasts. I'd dressed in the nicest clothes I had, which I realized as soon as I walked in were too nice, too revealing, too expensive.

The sermon dragged on forever, and the entire time he and I were making eyes at each other, trading I-wasn't-staring glances away. When the old woman sat down at the piano and dug into a horrific rendition of "Oh What A Friend We Have In Jesus", I bolted. I mean, I ran out of that church. I clicked down the steps in my too-high heels, stretching my legs as far as my too-tight skirt would let me.

He wasn't far behind, although I didn't dare look to see. I could feel him, though. His eyes were on my ass as I climbed the hill, and I gave my hips an extra sway on my way to the swing. The ropes were scratchy, fuzzy, generations-old hemp, the fibers sticking to my palms as I gripped them, and the weathered, gray wooden plank seat was rough, small, and hard under my bottom. I kicked my heels gently, giving me a little momentum. I kept my knees pressed together as he approached, the habit of a woman who's spent her life in skirts.

He made it up the hill and stood staring at me, mouth open a little as he hunted for words. I let my knees go apart, just a touch. I had to make myself do it though; my mind and my libido wanted me to let him get a glimpse, just a teasing look, but physical habit wanted me to keep my knees together.

My libido won.

His eyes darted to my thighs, to the little triangle of darkness between them. His zipper bulged out slightly, and I let my knees part a bit more. He was still looking for something to say, and I could see his hands shaking a little. Looking at him, then, I realized he wasn't just another congregation member; he had the same jaw and the same long nose as the pastor, the same towering height, although he was still lean and fit where the pastor was running to two or three spare tires around his middle. This was the pastor's son. The preacher's kid. My own father had been a preacher, before he died of a heart attack the year I left with Dan. I knew what PK's were like: sheltered, sequestered, kept innocent of the world and its wicked ways.

Kept away from women like me.

I took pity on his awkwardness. "Hi," I said, sticking out my hand.

"Hi." His voice didn't break, but it was pitched low, as if he was afraid to talk too loud.

He shook my hand gently, not limp and not crushing, just a gentle, firm touch. His eyes kept wandering to my cleavage, and I found myself arching my back to make my breasts look bigger, to give him a better show.

"I'm Shea," I said. "Shea Harley."

He smiled, a bright, amused grin. "Shea Harley? Wow, that's a cool name." He ducked his head, and a lock of black hair fell across his eye; I was already growing to adore that stray lock of hair and the thumb that brushed it aside. "I'm Tre."

He said it "Tray". I must've given him a curious look, because he shrugged his shoulders and looked embarrassed.

"It's a nickname. My initial are T-R-E: Timothy Robert Evan. I hate my name, so I go by Tre."

I kept swinging, letting my foot brush his leg at each apex. "I like that. Tre. It fits you so much better than Tim. You're definitely not a Tim." He shifted forward, and when I swung forward again, I let my foot slide up his calf to the back of his knee.

It was a first hesitant flirt, just to see how he'd react. He glanced at the offending foot, and then at me, as if wondering what I could mean by it, and what he was supposed to do in return. I could see him thinking, figuring, wondering.

"So, Tre. What do you do?"

He shrugged. "I work at a garage, changing oil and fixing cars and such. Daddy wants me to go to seminary, but I'm just not sure I want to. I ain't decided yet."

"Your dad's the preacher, right?"

"Yep. Although don't let him hear you call him 'Preacher'. He's a pastor, he says. He's got a whole lecture on how a pastor is called to the pulpit and his flock, but anyone can get up and preach."

"And you don't want to be a pastor?" I swung forward again, and this time I caught myself on his legs with my feet, hanging there by my hooked toes, and then swinging free again.

Tre shrugged again, but I could tell there was a lot on his mind, a lot expressed by that nonchalant shrug. "Not really. I just ain't felt the call, you know? I never been outside of Mississippi, and I've barely ever left Yazoo. I just...I don't know. Seems like there might be more out there for me than one little town, one little church, for all my life."

He fell silent, and he seemed embarrassed. I don't think he meant to say all that.

"Well, I think you oughta make your own choices," I said, standing up.

There was only two steps between us, and I took one so I was just inside his personal space. My breasts were nearly brushing his chest, and he was valiantly trying to keep his eyes on mine.

"You know, you're right about one thing, Tre. There is a whole world out there. You just never know what you might find." I fanned my face with my hand. "It sure is hot out here, isn't it?"

I had my blouse buttoned up to just above my cleavage, and the button at the bulge of my breasts was straining. I met his eyes, held them, and slowly, oh so slowly let my hand drift up to that button, touched it with my finger. Tre's tongue touched the corner of his lips, and I nearly kissed him then. He knew I was playing a game, so I kept playing it. He was waiting, and I drew the moment out. I circled the little white button with my index finger, then pinched it and pushed it through, tugged my blouse apart so an indecent of cleavage was revealed.

It took a lot longer for his burning mocha eyes to return to mine.

"You're hot," he blurted, then closed his eyes in acute embarrassment.

I laughed, shifting forward, closer to him. "Thank you, Tre. I think you're pretty hot, yourself."

He looked confused by this. "You do?"

I nodded. "Mmmmm-hmmm. I do. You're sexy." He blushed scarlet.

He seemed to be trying to come up with something else to say. "No one's ever told me that, before."

"Well, you are. If they all can't see that, well…they're blind." I was pressed up against him now, not crushed closed like I wanted to be, but nearly.

He was looking down at me, searching my eyes like they held some inscrutable secret. "I should probably go. My dad's gonna wonder where I'm at. We usually have lunch after sermon."

"Aww," I said, genuinely disappointed. "I was hoping to talk to you some more."

"You were?" He seemed shocked by that.

"Yeah, I was. Maybe you could come over to my house sometime, have some sweet tea with me."

He shifted his weight, obviously struggling with the decision.

After a long moment, he nodded. "I'm off work all day tomorrow."

I dug in my purse, pulled out an old gas station receipt and scribbled my address on it. He needed something bold, a gesture that'd hint at what I really wanted; I slipped the card into his back pocket, and I left my hand there, not squeezing—although lord knows I wanted to grope his tight ass—just resting in his pocket. I kissed him for good measure. It was a light thing, a peck on his lips, a lingering touch. He tensed, startled, and then parted his lips against mine, making the kiss into something more.

I pulled away first, and he looked disappointed.

"Why don't you swing by around lunchtime?" I said.

He just nodded, licking his lips, probably still tasting my lipstick. He looked shocked, both at me and at himself.

I hoped he'd show up the next day. I wanted to show him what he'd been missing all his life, and it sure as shit wasn't sweet tea I had in mind.

My own hunger surprised me. Watching him go, I felt a twinge of guilt; I was seducing a preacher's kid.

Two

He knocked, rather than ringing the doorbell. It was a light, hesitant knock. He was nervous, I could tell just by that. I went to the door, tugging my yellow sundress down, adjusting my breasts higher. My heart was hammering in my chest. I brushed a lock of my thick black hair back and smoothed my dress over my thighs, opened the door.

He was wearing tight blue jeans with a thick leather belt and a plain white T-shirt . Oh, my lord. His arms were brawny and bulging with the power of youth, and the shirt clung to his stomach. I felt desire pooling in my belly, turning to fire as his eyes devoured my body.

"You're here," I said.

It felt like a foolish thing to say, but he just nodded and stepped inside, brushing close to me.

"I'm here."

I took a deep breath and gathered myself. I wasn't really nervous so much as flushed with anticipation. I closed the door and put my back to it.

"Well, I'm glad you came." I took his hand, leaned in to kiss him.

He kissed me back, clumsy but ardent. I stepped into him, pressing my body up against him. He tensed and pulled away.

"I thought we were having sweet tea?"

I went for broke: "That was just to get you here. I do have sweet tea, but I had something else in mind."

His eyes darted around the foyer, to the kitchen, and last to the stairs. "You did? Like what?"

His confusion was so cute, so innocent. He couldn't quite believe the signals he was obviously receiving in spades. I ran my hands down his chest and back up, touching his cheek. I stared up into his eyes, trying to communicate too much with one little look.

"Well, Tre, it starts with kissing you," I said, and touched my lips to his jaw, then to his ear, then to his neck, still holding one of his hands.

I led that hand to my back and left it there. He took the cue, tentatively exploring my back, daring down my hip, hesitating there. I kept my eyes on his, smiled my encouragement and pushed my breasts against him. He took a deep breath and moved his hand around from my hip to my backside. I curled into his chest, put my hand to the soft thatch of hair at the back of his neck and pulled him down into a kiss, and this time I made it full and deep, putting a promise into it, slipping my tongue between his lips to touch his.

He pulled away and looked down at me. "What are we doing, Shea?"

I knew he was asking a whole bunch of things. His eyes showed the conflict: desire and guilt.

"I like you. I want you."

"You want me?" He licked his lips, eyes darting over my face and my eyes. "What do you mean, you want me? And why me?"

I laughed. "Why you? I don't know, other than....I like you. I think you're sexy, and I like kissing you. I want to kiss you more."

His eyebrows dug down, and I saw desire winning the war. I ground my hips into his, felt the hardening length of his penis through his jeans.

"Is it...should we...I mean..."

"Tre, if you don't think you should, then don't. I want you to want me, but if you don't, then you can go, and nobody will know anything different. So the question is, do you want me?"

"I—yeah, I do, but—"

"Do you like kissing me?"

"Well, yeah, I do, but—"

Time for the clincher: "Do you think kissing me is wrong? Is that what you're afraid of?" He nodded.

"Don't be afraid, Tre. Remember how we talked about making your own choices?"

He nodded again, thinking. I could feel the decision clicking into place.

"Make this choice for you, for what you want. It's not about your father, or your future. It's just about you and me," I said. "If you want to go, you can. I'll still be your friend, and I won't be mad or anything. But I would like it if you stayed with me."

His hands both moved to my ass, squeezed, caressed, explored, and he kissed me. "I'll stay," he said, his voice husky.

"Good," I said. "I was hoping you would."

"I'm a little nervous," he said.

"That's okay," I told him. "You're allowed to be. But you don't have to be."

I took him by the hand and led him upstairs to my bedroom, let him stop in the French doorway and take in my room, my king size four-poster bed and the wide window overlooking a field of wildflowers. I led him down the three steps and stood in front of him at the foot of the bed.

I turned around and presented my back, pulling my hair over a shoulder. "Why don't you unzip my dress for me?"

He took the zipper with two trembling fingers and drew it downward, slowly. I stood still and let him go at his own pace. When the zipper was at my waist, put his hands on my bare shoulders and pushed the straps off, letting the dress fall to the floor. I turned around and let him look at me.

"It's okay to look at me," I told him.

"You're so beautiful," he said. "I've never seen a woman like...like this. Like you."

"I know," I said. "Would you like to see more?"

He flushed and smiled in response, and I turned back around.

"Take off my bra, then," I said.

He fumbled with bra, the four hook-and-eyelets frustrating his attempts to free them. He huffed, in embarrassment or frustration.

"It's okay," I said. "Take your time. It can be tricky if you've never done it before."

Finally, he got the bra free and it fell off, freeing my heavy breasts. I turned around to face him, standing in a barely-there red lace thong to match the bra. His eyes were about to pop out of his head. I stood still and let him look for a long moment before I pressed myself against him.

"Touch me," I said. "You can touch me everywhere. I want you to."

His cock pushed against my belly, a huge, hard bulge against the zipper of his jeans. I kissed his chin, and then his lips. He deepened the kiss on his own this time. We were lost, then, mouths apart and tongues delving. His hands began to roam over my body, stroking down my spine to my ass, feeling the curve and tracing the crack, hefting the individual globes and moving down my hips and back up to my breasts, crushed between us.

I pulled away and lifted his shirt over his head, tossing it aside. His abs were a wonderland of male perfection, toned and hard, dusted with a trail of hair down into his boxers. I reached with both hands to unbutton his jeans, unzipped them as slowly as I could, pushed them down to his feet. He stepped out of them and kicked them aside. His cock was leaking pre-come, moistening his boxers, pressing up against the fabric. He looked down at himself, and seemed embarrassed by the touch of wetness there.

I touched the wet spot. "Don't worry about that. It's normal."

He nodded and touched my nipples, lifted my breast in a hand.

I wanted to shock him, make him understand my own desire for him. "I want to see your cock," I said. "I want to feel you. You're gorgeous, Tre, do you know that?"

He just shook his head, unable to speak. I curled my fingers inside the band of his boxers and pulled them away from his body, glancing in. I looked up at him and grinned my delight at what I saw, then giggled at the terrified expression on his face. I pulled the flannel-print fabric down around his hips, tugging slowly by the bottom hem, freeing his cock in slow increments. Then, with a sudden rush, they fell to the ground and his penis was free, standing straight up against his belly, wet at the head, throbbing and undulating with his breathing. He was huge, thick and long and straight, and so, so beautiful.

I touched the glistening tip, licked the pre-come off my finger, my eyes locked on his. Then I grabbed him, first with one hand, pumping slowly, then the other, both hands around his pulsating girth and still the tip stood above my hands.

"You are so huge," I told him. "Your cock is perfect. I want it inside me. I want it my pussy. I want it in my mouth."

He laughed, nervous and disbelieving, his hips moving in time with my hands. He was so close, already. His knees were about to buckle.

"Your mouth? You would really do that? Put your mouth on my...on my—"

"Say it," I commanded, leading him to the bed. "Say a dirty word for me."

He lay down on his back, cupping my breasts as I sat astride him, still wearing my panties. I knew he wouldn't last long enough to even get inside, and I wanted to milk him, feel his cock in my hands and see his face as he came. This was just the beginning.

"You'd really put my...cock in your mouth?"

"Oh Tre...there's so much I'm going to do you." I slid downward, taking him in my hands again. "This is just the very beginning of all the things I'm going to do to you."

He gasped when I licked him, his stomach pulling in as I laved the silky, salty length of his shaft from the base up to the tip, swirling my tongue around his sensitive head. I cupped his balls in my hand, used my other to grasp him again, sliding my fist around him, tickling him with a gentle fingernail. I kissed the wet head, pink and soft, and then wrapped my lips around him, taking him in an inch at first, then moved back out.

"I feel like I'm going to explode," he said, his voice a panting whisper.

"Haven't you ever jerked off before?"

"Yeah, but it ain't never felt like this before," he gasped. "My dad always told me it was a sin to touch myself except to pee."

He was rocking his hips as I moved my hands on his length, slow as molasses, milking the pleasure for him. I wanted this moment to be burned in his mind forever.

"Do you like this? Do you like it when I put my mouth on your cock?"

He nodded, desperate. "Yes, oh god...it feels amazing." He looked down at me, his eyes hooded. "You're sure it's not gross for you?"

"No, Tre. I like it. I love your cock. It's so big. After you come in my mouth, I'm going to show you how to make me feel as good as you do."

He nodded, and rolled his hips. I had his balls in

one hand and I was massaging them gently, not touching his cock, letting him back away from the edge of orgasm. Now I took him in both hands, licking the tip in quick circles, pumping up and down until he was grinding against me furiously. I took him in my mouth, slipped him in inch by inch, still moving my hands on him, sucking until he was against the back of my throat. I spat him out and sucked him back in slowly, and now he was groaning, arching his back, and his hips were rocking and I was matching his motion, and then he cried out and shot his seed into my throat, hot and salty and thick, almost sweet.

I kept my hands on him, moving on his pulsing member to draw out his orgasm until he was locked in an arch. After a moment, I let go and moved up next to him, snuggling my head against his shoulder, rubbing his stomach with my hand.

"Did you like that?"

He could only nod, and gasp. "Yes," he said, when had his breath back. "Oh my god, yes. I didn't know nothing could feel that way. It was like I was on fire and then I exploded, and...oh god."

I laughed. "Good. I'm glad."

"Shea? What happened to the...to what came out?"

I giggled against his shoulder. "Your semen? I swallowed it. It tasted good."

He didn't know what to say to that, so he didn't say anything.

Then: "Now what?"

I giggled again. "Oh Tre. You're cute, and so innocent. I'll change that." I pulled at his shoulder, rolling
him toward me. "Now you touch me. Kiss me."

He moved for my lips, and I kissed him, then
pushed him away. "No, Tre, I meant my body. I want to
feel your lips on my body. All over."

He looked down at me. "Everywhere?"

I just nodded, biting my lower lip in anticipation of
his mouth on me.

He lifted up on an elbow and his gaze raked down
my body to my panties and the damp spot on them. I
wanted him inside me, I wanted his cock to be hard
again and to plunge into me, but I had to wait a few
minutes more, at least. I took his free hand in mine and
moved it to my breasts.

"Everywhere. Touch me and kiss me at the same
time. Take my tits in your mouth. Play with my nipples.
Do everything. Do anything. Touch me everywhere."

He didn't need any further encouragement. His
fingers took my stiffened nipple in his and rolled it,
pinched it, not too hard, then he slid his palm along my
ribs to my hips, touched a tickling finger to my thighs
and traced up to touch the triangle of the panties.

"Do you like my body, Tre?" I asked him.

I was asking as much to hear the validation as to
encourage him.

"Yes, Shea." He kissed his lips to my stomach, put

his tongue to my nipple and licked me, suckled me. "I love your body. I'd imagined what a woman looked like naked, but you, you're like...I don't know how to put it. You're perfect."

He tugged on the panties, and I lifted my hips to let him draw them off. His eyes widened when he saw my shaved pussy, wet with the juices of my desire. His fingers found my cleft and touched the line of my labia, then my clit. I gasped when his index finger touched my clit.

"Yes, yes, just like that. Put your fingers in my pussy." I put my hands on his and pushed his fingers inside, helped him circle my wet, sensitive nub.

"You like it when I touch you like this?" he said.

"I like it as much as you liked it when I touched your cock."

He suckled my nipple and stroked my clit, bringing me up and up and up into a frenzy, moaning and gasping, bucking my hips as he fondled me. I guided his hands, showing him how to build me up and then slow down. He moved his finger in and found my G-spot by accident, and when I whimpered in pleasure he rubbed it with a long finger, drawing a gasp from me. So close, I was so close, yes, and then I was there, fire blooming in my pussy and spreading to my belly and sending ecstasy through me in a crescendo of waves.

I curled around him, clutched him, kissed him, tasting the musk of his come in my mouth still, tasting his salt on my lips, reveling in the hard planes and contours of his body. I shuddered against him, roaming his stomach and hips and ass with my hands, raking him with my fingers as aftershocks rumbled through me.

"Oh...Tre..." I breathed, "that was so wonderful, thank you."

He kissed me, caressed me everywhere his hands could reach. "I never knew there could be feelings like that." He nipped my neck, tasting me, then pulled back and looked down at me. "Shea? What did it taste like? You really didn't mind putting my cock in your mouth?"

I smiled against him. "No. I liked it. I promise you I'm telling the truth. I liked being able to do that to you, showing you how good it could feel." I slipped my hand down his stomach to the hard V where his hips met his groin, felt him suck his belly in as I took his flaccid cock in my hands, rolling it, fondling the head in my fingers, rubbing him with my thumb and stroking him. Almost immediately I felt him grow hard. I was eager to feel him inside me, to feel him fill me.

Oh, my lord, I knew he would fill me so full.

I pinched his nipples, kissed them, nipped them with my teeth, cupped his sack with my hand, massaged his taint with my fingers and toyed with his now-rigid cock, until he was moist and throbbing in my hands.

He was ready, then, and I slid astride him, placing my palms on his chest and gazing down at him.

"Are you ready?" I asked him.

He nodded, took my hips in his hands and pulled me towards him, eager, still a little nervous. I leaned forward over him, crushing my breasts against him and lifting my hips up. I guided him toward my folds, wetter than ever with anticipation and desire. His eyes were hooded and burning, and his breath was coming in long, deep gasps.

"Wait, Shea. Wait."

What? You don't want to?" I sat back on his legs. "That's okay, we can wait—"

"No, I do want to. Just..." He touched my belly with a finger. "What if you get pregnant?"

I leaned down and kissed him, impressed by his consideration. "Tre, it's wonderful that you thought of that before we did it. Please don't ask any questions right now, but I can't get pregnant. I'm healthy and fine and everything, I just can't conceive, okay? You don't need to worry. And I'm also clean...meaning I don't have any diseases you could catch."

Tre seemed shocked by that last consideration, then he shrugged and tugged at my hips. "Okay, then. If you're sure it's okay."

"It's more than okay," I said. "I can't wait any longer. I want you inside me, Tre."

I kissed him, flicking my tongue against his, guided him inside me, slow, so slow. He was bigger than I had imagined, I realized as I slid him into my pussy, inch by inch by inch, gasping, panting, quivering my mouth against his, until he was buried into me to the hilt, hips grinding against hips. Tre was breathing hard already, fluttering his pelvis against mine desperately.

"Slow, Tre...slow..."

I rocked my hips up, pulling him out so only his head was inside, and then lowered down again, impaling myself on him again, loving every slip of skin against skin.

"Oh, god, Tre," I breathed into his ear, "You feel so good inside me. You're so big...you fill me...oh god, yes, don't stop....just like that..."

Tre fell into the rhythm I was setting, long, slow strokes, his hands rubbing my back, my ass, my neck, brushing aside my hair to kiss my lips and my neck and my clavicle. I wanted to thrust down on him hard and fast, but I held back, savoring every moment. His hands were strong and gentle, and his motions rhythmic and confident, more sure with every passing second, especially as I began to moan in pleasure.

I'd never been vocal during sex before, but then I'd never felt anything like him, never been so filled, so satisfied by a man. I let myself go, let my wet pussy slap against his balls, collapsed against his chest and pumped my hips, crying out against his lips.

His orgasm began to rise and his voice joined mine, raised in ecstasy to fill the room with our merged cries of pleasure. Something told me he was holding back, though, something in the way he was carefully matching my rhythm, even as I could tell he was near coming.

"Don't hold back." I told him, meeting his eyes. "Please, don't hold back. I want it hard, now. Fast. Fuck me hard."

He actually gasped when I swore, and I laughed, not mocking him, but amused.

"Say that. Say it for me."

He let himself go, burying his face in my neck, putting his hands on my hips and pulling me down onto him as he railed into me, hard, hard, hard, furious now, no rhythm or restraint. It drove me even wilder.

"I love fucking you, Shea," he said, his voice a guttural rasp against my throat. "Don't stop, please don't stop."

"Come with me, Tre," I said. "I'm so close."

"I am too, I'm about to explode."

"Tell me you're gonna come inside me. Tell me you're gonna come deep inside my pussy."

My words had the desired effect, driving him to a frenzy, grunting and heaving his breath against me, which only made me crazier as well. I was full of him, feeling his cock thrum against my cervix, pounding me, driving me into abandon.

Then he shuddered, paused, thrust hard into me, once—pause, gasping groan—twice, three times— "I'm coming, Shea...I'm...I'm coming deep inside your pussy."

I couldn't speak then, driven to orgasm now myself, explosion after explosion rocking through me as he continued to drive into me, still coming, a flood of hot seed against my inner walls and even when his load was spent he kept plunging hard into me, wild thrusts split by a pause and his hands on my hips jerking me down onto him. I was shrieking into his pectoral, clawing his shoulders, fluttering my pussy around his relaxing cock, softening and still pulsing inside me.

"Oh, God," I whispered. "You are so good. That was amazing....so incredible."

Tre only panted, his hands supporting my limp weight on his body. "Did I die and go to heaven?"

I laughed. "Yes, you did. I'm your personal sex-angel. I'm here to see that you feel that kind of pleasure forever."

"Oh, good," he said. "Can we do that again? Soon?"

I slipped him out of me and laid next to him.

I nodded. "We can do that all the time. But there's so much else, so many other ways."

"Other ways?" His confused awe made me giggle again.

"Oh lord, Tre. Yes, there's a million ways. You can be on top, or we can be on our sides, or I can put my legs over your shoulders, or standing up, or in the car..."

I played idly with his limp cock, amazed at how much it grew from this flaccid state into the glorious, perfect specimen of male anatomy it was when fully hard. I was lying partially on my side, and I rolled on to my belly next to him. I took his hand and moved it down to my ass, left it there and pushed my hips up.

"You can even put it in there, you know. You can touch me there, too. Just be slow and gentle. Dip your fingers in my pussy and get them wet, first."

He hesitated. "In your butt?"

"Yes, in my asshole. I won't let you hurt me. It will feel good."

He hesitated still, and I took his hand, dipped his fingers into my come-dripping folds and led them to my back door. He pushed his index finger in, slowly, gently, carefully. I guided him, moving his finger in and out, gasping into the pillow, watching him from the corner of my eyes, loving the marvel in his expression.

"You like it?" he asked.

"Yes...just like that..." I said. I took his cock in my hand, pumped him, fondled him.

I just couldn't get enough, couldn't be satisfied. After so long of nothing, just boredom and ridicule, Tre's sweet, ardent passion was exactly what I wanted.

Tre leaned over me and slid his other hand between my legs, underneath his slowly-sliding finger and touched my pussy again.

"Higher," I told him. "Touch my clit, near the top. Yeah, right there."

He found the spot, circled it, massing my clit gently in circles. He moved his hands at the same slow pace, matching their rhythm, increasing it when I started to pant and rock my hips again. His cock was growing hard yet again, and oh my sweet lord the man was a machine, ready again so soon. I came, more convulsive explosions one after another, tightening my anus around his finger.

I pushed his hand away from my ass and rolled to my back. "Take me again, Tre, I want it so bad."

I pulled him on top of me, spread my legs and wrapped them high around his back, lifting my head up to watch him carefully slide his cock back inside me. He was being so gentle, so careful, so sweet. It made my heart clench and throb, and I had a fleeting fear mixed with equal parts hope that this tryst might become something else, something more.

There were no thoughts, then, just his huge cock inside me for the second time.

"Don't hold back. Take me all you want, take me as hard as you want. Don't be gentle. Just fuck me."

He rocked into me, flicking my nipples, then kissing them and sucking my breast into his mouth as he moved inside me. I was still throbbing from my last orgasm, my third, and now with him inside me yet again, I felt it rising up, wetness pooling around him until we were both dripping, sloppy and messy and hot and moving together, my nails raking his back, my hips bucking against his.

He lost control, then, and I loved it. Loved it, so much. He was rocking into me, thrusting wildly, madly, grunting, slapping his balls into me, his fists planted to either side of my head, and then his weight pressed down on me and he was moving just his hips, slowing down, slowing, a pause with him pressed hard hips to hips, gasping, crying out loud against my breasts.

"Oh, yes, harder, harder," I said.

He went hard again, plunging a slow crashing thrust into me, once, twice, a third time, and then I took over, screaming into his shoulder and my entire body was ripped into shreds of pleasure, an agony of ecstasy.

He collapsed on top of me, and we both passed out.

I woke up to a fist pounding on my door, and a deep voice calling out, "Mrs. Harley!"

Tre jerked awake. "That's my dad!"

Three

I left the bed and donned a robe from the bathroom, a thin, silky flower-print thing that came to my knees. I knotted it tight so my breasts were covered, hidden. I tried to pretend my heart wasn't knocking in my chest just as loudly as Pastor McNabb's fist was on my door.

"Stay here," I told Tre.

I pulled the door open. "Can I help you?" I asked.

"Where is my son?" It was a harsh demand, no Southern politeness here, just angry brown eyes and sweating jowls.

"Can I help you, Pastor McNabb?" I repeated, trying to force myself to coolness.

"I want to know where my son is!"

"Well, I'm not sure why you would come pounding on my door, then. If that's all..." I trailed off and started to push the door shut.

His hand caught the door and he began pushing past me. "He's here, woman. His truck is in your driveway. I saw you talking to him after sermon yesterday. Don't play games with me, not about my boy." Brian McNabb was furious, jabbing a finger in my face.

"Excuse me, Pastor. This is my home, and I have not invited you in," I said, pushing him back out the door. "You can leave now. I have no reason to answer your questions. Your concerns regarding your son's whereabouts have nothing to do with me."

The pastor stood in the doorway, seething. "You seduced my boy, woman. You ruined him. I know he's in there, up in your bedroom, your...your den of iniquity." He spat on the ground at his feet. "You just tell my son he ain't welcome in my home no more. You tell him that...*harlot*. He made his choice, now he's gotta live with it."

I noticed his accent, so carefully cultivated to be charming and reassuring in the pulpit, had taken on a different tone, now. I regarded him with an icy glare, hoping he couldn't see the pounding of my pulse in my throat.

What had I done?

"Pastor McNabb, you are out of line. You are barging in here, into my home, making accusations, calling me names, and publicly disowning your son when you have no facts, no evidence, besides your son's vehicle in my driveway." I jabbed my finger at him, as he'd done to me. "You are rude, uncouth, and unwelcome. Please leave. Now."

He turned and stormed off, stopping at the sidewalk and facing me once more. "You tell him what I said, Mrs. Harley. I meant it. I know the truth, and so do you. You tell him."

I watched him drive away in his rattling old forest-green Cadillac, and then shut the door. Tre was standing just out of sight, on the middle of the stairs. He wasn't crying, but he was clearly distraught.

I crossed over to him, took him by the hand and led him into the kitchen. Wearing just his jeans, zipped but unbuttoned and showing that sexy V of muscle and a hint of the thatch of curly black hairs, I felt a flood of desire for him, even as the gravity of the situation permeated the air between us.

He sat down at the island, perching on the stool, shoulders slumped, forehead buried in his hands.

"What did I do?" he said. "What did I do?"

I put my hands on his shoulders, standing behind him. I kissed his back between his shoulder blades, feeling a tenderness for him that I shouldn't have, not so soon, not when this was supposed to be just...

I trailed off the thought, in my head, realizing I really hadn't considered what this relationship might be, when I invited him here. I just knew I wanted him, and that an afternoon of sex with him would go a long way to helping me realize I had really started my life over.

And now, suddenly, I had ruined this young man's life.

"You made a choice, Tre," I said. "I don't know your dad, but he may come around. You never know. And if not...Well, if he's so easily able to disown you for one little choice like this, then I just have to question his... not his love, but his ability to accept you."

"He won't come around," Tre said, his voice low and miserable.

"Maybe not," I said. "But, you know...if you're gonna make your own decisions in life, it probably would have come to this at some point. If you decided not to do what your father had planned for you, he'd have gotten angry and told you to do what you wanted anyways and to not come back."

Tre nodded, rubbing his eyes. "Yeah, you're right. He's had my life planned since I was born, and I've never had much say in that. Working at the garage, that's been a big fight for years, ever since I told him I wasn't going to seminary after high school. Now, well...I don't know what I'll do."

I sat on the stool next to him, loosening the robe a little. "Do you regret it?" I asked him. "Do you regret what we did together?"

He took a long moment to answer, honestly considering.

"No, I don't," Tre said. "I made the choice, and I don't regret it. It was the most amazing experience of my life, and I can't believe it was wrong. Maybe it was, but I don't care."

"Good," I said. "We'll figure this out. And listen, if you want to try to work things out with your dad, I understand. I mean, if you have to...to not see me, to work it out, then I understand."

He looked at me, his gaze mature and understanding. He seemed to sense how hard that was for me to say.

He shook his head, saying, "No, that won't work, even if I wanted to try. Even if I crawled back to him and begged him to forgive me, and promised to never see you again and did everything he said, he still wouldn't let it go. It'd always be there between us."

He turned to face me, putting his knees on either side of mine, his gaze flowing over my body, taking in my hair, still sleep-mussed, and down my neckline to my breasts peeking out of the robe, to my crotch, visible to him as I sat with my feet on the rung of the stool, knees apart a little.

"So now what?" I asked. "What do you want? You're welcome to stay here, of course, for as long as you want."

He shrugged, a gesture of not knowing rather than not caring. "I don't know. I don't have anything here, not even a toothbrush or a change of boxers. I can't just hide out in here, never coming out." He grinned at me, flirting. "Although I might enjoy being holed up in here with you..."

"But we both have lives to live."

He nodded. "You know everyone will know, now. Everyone will be talking. They already are right now, since Mrs. Henderson must have seen me drive by and not drive back. There's only one house past hers, and she'd do the math, come to the same conclusions as Daddy."

I grimaced. "Don't call him that. I know it's a Southern thing, but it seems weird to me, a grown man calling his father 'Daddy.'"

Tre shrugged again. "Okay." He slipped his hand onto my thigh, sliding it up and back down. "I don't care about people, right now. I know they'll talk. I don't care."

"This is your home, Tre...and I just wanted to say I'm sorry you're in trouble on my account."

He moved closer still, moving his hand to my hip, spreading the robe apart. "I'm not. You said it yourself: this was coming, one way or another. This just sped it up a bit."

I sat still, letting him touch me, letting him explore me with his hands and his eyes. When his fingers moved down between my legs, I scootched back off the stool and out of his reach.

"Not just yet," I said. "First, we need to eat. You need your strength, you know."

He grinned. "I am hungry."

I made sandwiches and served him coffee while he waited, sipping my own while I slathered mayo and layered cheese and ham. We devoured the meal, munching on chips.

He seemed deep in thought as he ate, and I elbowed him. "What's up, buttercup?"

He shrugged. "Just wondering. Why can't you have kids? If you don't want to talk about it, I get it. I'm just wondering."

I took a deep breath and let it out. "That's a long story, Tre. It's long and depressing and old history. I'll tell you some time, I promise. For now, lets just say that I got sick, and things...stopped working like they should. I'm not sick anymore, so you don't have to worry."

He nodded. "Okay, well, tell me when you're ready."

We finished eating, and I led him back upstairs. This time, though, I had something else in mind. I took him into the bathroom, took off my robe and hung it up. I started the shower, letting it turn steamy hot while I helped Tre out of his jeans.

"I need a shower," I told him. "A lady needs to get clean after making love to her man."

Tre nodded, devouring my naked body with his eyes, but kept his hands at his side. He was ready, his cock standing straight up to his belly button as he stood in front of me, just waiting. I let him wait, enjoying a moment of pure ogling.

He was hot as hell, standing there, hard for me, wreathed in steam, muscles growing damp from the moisture in the air until he glistened. Eventually I stepped into the shower, gesturing for him to follow me. I got my hair wet and switched places with Tre so he was beneath the water jet, and I admired the way his muscles moved as he lathered his hair. When his eyes closed to rinse his hair, I took his softening penis in my hand, and he jerked in surprise, then relaxed. He went rigid immediately, and I laughed, taking the bar of soap in my hand and rubbing it against his chest.

"I love how you get hard so fast," I said.

I soaped him up, rubbing my water-slick body against him as I did so, and he caught on, taking the soap from me and rubbing it between my breasts, slipping in little circles down my stomach and swiping it across my back, kissing me as he leaned over me, reaching around to move the soap on my ass, down the crack to the creases of each thigh.

Tre ground his hips against my belly, wanting inside me. I held him in my hand, pumping him, getting him going. He leaned back against the shower wall, and I lowered myself to my knees. He looked down at me, head leaning back. I smiled up at him, licking the tip of his cock. He took a deep breath, closed his eyes as I rubbed my thumb in circles on the tip, drawing the pre-come from him. I took him in my mouth, then, all the way, as far as I could, bobbing with him deep inside. He was long enough that even with him at the back of my throat I had enough room on his silk-steel length to wrap my fingers around him. I took his testicles in my hand, rubbed his taint as I sucked him, spat him out, sucked him again. I drew my mouth off to pump him with both hands, now, putting just my lips on the bulbous head. He arched his back, and his knees buckled as he came. His hands drifted to my hair, taking its sopping weight in his hands and stroking my scalp as I continued to bob on him until he was groaning, pushing his cock into my mouth with throbs of pleasure.

I helped him sit down on the floor, the water raining down on us. When he had his breath back, he looked at me, a question in his eyes.

"Shea? I was wondering something. Earlier, while we were together, you kept telling me to fuck you," he said the word with less hesitation, this time, and I could tell he was a little proud of it. "But just now, you said we were making love. So, my question is, is there a difference to you in what the words mean?"

I stood up to wash and condition my hair as I answered. "Well, that's a complicated question, and really depends on who you're talking to. For me, it depends on context, usually. During, like before, I told you to fuck me, and I used that word to talk dirty to you. I just meant it to...I don't know...encourage you, I guess.

To let you know I liked what you were doing. But if was to talk about our relationship, in a more general sense, I'd use a different word. I'd call it making love, or having sex, and that's it. When it's not during sex, I don't like calling it fucking because that seems cheap, or something."

Tre nodded. "That makes sense." He went silent again, just staring down at me, his expression serious. "Do we have a relationship?"

I froze. I wasn't ready for that discussion yet.

"Let's not worry about categories just yet, Tre. Okay? I mean, do we have to put it into a neat little box? I like you, a lot. I like spending time with you, just like this, or just eating sandwiches, or making love to you. I want to get to know you, find out about you. But...I just don't think we need any categories, just yet."

"So it's...casual, then?" He was trying to sound nonchalant, worldly.

I took his face in my hands and kissed him, deeply.

"No, Tre. No. Casual would mean we were seeing other people, seeing other people besides each other. That's not what I want, and it's not what I meant."

He nodded, relieved.

"Then what did you mean?"

I wished he wasn't so relentless in this topic, but I couldn't blame him.

"I don't know. How's that for honest? I don't know. I don't know what I want with you besides to spend time together, okay?"

He seemed to sense he was pushing me in some way, and he nodded, brushing a sopping tendril of my hair away from my cheek.

We got out, dried off, and wrapped up in towels. He followed me downstairs to the kitchen and sat down, waiting. I guess he knew I had something in mind. I took a pair of beers from my fridge, handing them to him to twist off. He lifted an eyebrow, and then wrenched the tops free.

"Since you're trying new things..." I said, lifting my bottle to him in a toast.

He clinked the bottles and took a long swig, longer than I'd expected. This wasn't his first beer.

"Me and Jimmy sneak beers all the time. Jimmy's dad drinks and don't notice when we take some."

We drank our beers in the living room on my tan suede couch, chatting as the sun went down. I told him about growing up in Savannah as a preacher's daughter, and he told me about his adventures with his friend Jimmy, hunting, fishing, hiking out into the wilderness and once getting hopelessly lost in the woods for two days. We drank a second, and a third, and that was when he started to slur a bit. I was sloppy myself by then, never having been a hard drinker.

I kissed him, suddenly. He nearly dropped his beer, then reached over and placed it on the coffee table. We'd been wrapped in our towels the whole time, and I untucked the edge of his towel, lifted it free and set it aside. He did the same to me, and I pushed him down on the couch, onto his back, laying on top of him, lifting my hips to push him deep inside me.

We took it slow, then, moving our hips in a slow roll, arms wrapped tight around each other, bodies clenched close. He kept it slow, even as he rose to orgasm, forcing himself to keep it slow, and I felt a pang of deep affection for him for that. He lasted, and lasted, and when he started to come and I wasn't ready, he slowed, stopped, gritting his teeth and straining every muscle in his body to hold back. I kept still, awed at his control, the strength it took to hold back like that, especially when he was still so new at all this.

I came hard, biting his shoulder, and he released into me, clutching my ass to himself as he exploded, sighing in pleasure.

We made love again and again that night, usually with me on top, until Tre was too exhausted to move, and I was sore in all the right ways. Dawn came and found us just falling asleep.

Four

Tre strode confidently up the door of his father's house, arms swinging wide, gait easy, back straight.

He'd decided as we ate a late breakfast—late being past noon—that he had to at least talk to his dad once. I agreed, and admired him all the more for the courage I knew it must take to face his father.

I offered to go in with him, present a united front, which was a difficult thing to offer, but he refused, saying it was between him and his dad, and it wasn't really about me at all. I admit I was relieved, and sat in the passenger seat of his truck, watching him go. I was proud of him, and scared for him.

Most of all, I wondered where the hell this relationship was going. I'd only been in Yazoo for two weeks and I was already bored. I was glad I'd rented the house instead of buying it like I'd considered doing. If things with Tre continued, we'd be the scandal of the town, and I had no desire to stay and be the fodder for gossip. I wasn't sure I was ready to take Tre with me, though. I went in circles while I waited, weighing my options against my desires.

Nearly an hour passed before Tre came out again, anger written in every line of his face, in the aggressive stomp of his boots.

"Bastard," he said as he sat down in the driver's seat. "Stubborn old goat. I didn't expect any different, but still, it hurts. And it pisses me off. I'm so angry at him I could spit nails, I swear."

I took his hand, twined our fingers, not speaking. He didn't need my words, just my presence. He let me hold his hand as he drove, heading not toward my house but somewhere else, outside of town in a direction I'd not explored yet.

"Where're we going?" I asked.

"I thought we'd hang out with Jimmy. I want to introduce you. He's my only real friend, and the only person left who cares about me."

I realized then that I'd never seen his mom, or heard him talk about her. "What about your mom?"

His shoulders tensed. "She's just...there. She don't stick up for me, or care much. I don't know. She's just there. It don't matter."

His accent always got more pronounced when he was upset. I placed our twined fingers on my leg and let him drive, kept the silence. Sometimes a man just has to stew.

Jimmy Dixon was the opposite of Tre in every way. Short, thick, with long brown greasy hair held back in a ponytail, Jimmy was a nice guy, shaking my hand and appraising me appreciatively. We sat in an old barn and drank beer and talked, and Tre sat beside me, his arm around me, trying to act casual.

I decided to show off a little, for Tre's sake. He wanted to impress his friend, and I thought I'd oblige. When we all finished our beer, I offered to get more and as I came back to pass them around, I sat down on Tre's lap, draping myself across him. He cast his eyes towards mine, smiling at me, letting me know he knew what I was doing.

Jimmy looked away, and I saw jealousy in his eyes, a flash and then gone.

We spent the day with Jimmy, heading back to my house as the sun set.

Instead of getting out with me, Tre stayed in the truck. "I'm going to grab a few things from home...from my parent's house. I'll be back in a little bit."

I agreed, kissed him, told him to be careful. I'd seen the anger in both men, and I didn't want Tre to come back hurt.

He showed up about half an hour later, bringing big duffel bag upstairs with him, anger and frustration and hurt in his eyes and the set of his jaw. He stopped short when he saw me. I'd decided to surprise him with a little show, a reward for standing up to his dad. I was lying on the bed, posing. I was on my side, facing the doorway, head propped in one hand, wearing nothing but a long string of pearls I'd inherited from my grandmother. The pearls were draped around my neck and hanging between my breasts.

Tre just stood there for a shocked moment, staring at me. He dropped the bag and descended the three steps into my room—our room. He stood in front of me, his gaze openly ravenous.

"Take off your clothes," I told him. He started to oblige, ripping his shirt over his head.

"No. Slow. Give me a show," I said. "You like to look at me...well I like to look at you, too."

Tre smiled a slow smile and peeled his shirt off gradually, undulating his hips and rocking his torso. He moved awkwardly at first, hesitant and self-conscious, then gradually began to get into the dance. It wasn't a striptease like you'd see at stripclub, since he'd never seen that kind of dancing in movies or real life, but he gave it all he had, trying to dance sexily, and oh my Lord, did he succeed.

He wrapped his shirt around his fists and stretched his arms above his head, straining his muscles, posing, flexing. Then he tossed the shirt aside and unbuttoned his jeans, moving his hips in a suggestive circle. He turned around and faced away from me as he bent over to take off his shoes and socks, then turned back around and resumed his undulation of his abdominal muscles and the rocking of his hips. He pushed his pants off, sliding them down and stepping out, kicking them aside and dancing all the while.

It was a strange scene, his not-quite-comically cute dancing, still somehow sexy to me. His body turned me on, just the sight of his muscles and his cock bulging against his boxers. He teased me with his boxers, pulling them down and then back up, giving me peeks at his penis.

He stepped close to the bed, and I snagged the band of his boxers, rolling to my belly and pulling him to my face. I pushed the boxer down and took the head in mouth, sucking gently, a tease, a promise.

I pulled him onto the bed, pushed him onto his back and left him there.

"Do you trust me?" I asked.

He nodded, suddenly wary.

"I'm going to do something new tonight. Just lay there and let me do it. You'll like it, I promise."

He just nodded. I went to my dresser and pulled out two silk scarves, one crimson and one deep purple. I draped one scarf across his chest, took his right hand in mine, wrapped the end of the scarf around his wrist and tied the other end to the bedpost, wrapping it around both post and wrist several times and tying it off. I sat astride him, taking the other scarf in my hand. I ground my pussy against him, getting him ready, sliding my slick, desire-wet flesh against him.

"Oh, please," he whispered. "I want you."

He reached for me, slid his free hand over me, touching my breasts and nipples, stretching down to reach for my pussy.

"You'll have me," I said, grinding against him but not sheathing him inside me yet. "But I'm not done tying you up. You'll just have to trust me."

He rocked his hips against me once more, caressed my breast before lying back and waiting. I tied his left wrist like the right.

"Are they too tight? It shouldn't hurt, just restrain you."

He shook his head. "No, it's fine. But how am I supposed to do anything like this?"

I laughed, sitting astride him again, but across his knees, leaving his body exposed to my hands. "You'll just have to let me do all the work, then, won't you?"

I ran my hands over him, tickling his thighs, cupping his balls and stroking his hard, silky length with a finger, then leaned over him and brushed my breasts up his body to kiss him. I slid against him, kissing him with all the passion I had, grinding against him until he was rocking into me in a desperate frenzy. I slid back away, then, leaving his cock wet and throbbing in open air, bending to kiss his hips, his thighs, kissing his sac and his cock before moving away to his belly again, planting soft, tonguing kisses all over his body.

I pressed my nipple into his mouth, let him suck my tits, switching back and forth, ignoring his still-thrusting hips. I moved up farther still, sitting on his chest, then up farther again and holding myself aloft by the posts.

"Kiss me, down there," I told him. "Lick my pussy."

I lowered my crotch to his face and felt his tongue lap out, stroking my entrance. I sighed in pleasure as he laved again, seeking my clit with the tip of his tongue, moving it in circles like I'd shown him to do with his fingers. I couldn't hold myself up for long, and slid back down his body until the head of his cock was pressed against my cleft.

"Will you do that to me again, later?" I asked.

"You tasted good, I liked it. I'll do it again. I'll do it all the time."

"Good," I breathed.

I took him in my hand and guided him in, just an inch at first. I fluttered my hips, quick, shallow thrusts, balancing upright so his cock was stretched away from his body. When his breathing began to grow ragged and his thrusts desperate, I pulled back up and away so he was nearly out of me, leaning forward then and holding there, just the very tip inside me. He was quivering, shaking, trying to get deeper, and I matched his forward thrusts with equal movements away. With each flutter of his tip, he throbbed against my clit, and I ground my teeth to contain my gasps, already so close, so near to coming.

"You're teasing me," Tre said.

"Yes, I am. I'm gonna draw this out until you can't stand it anymore."

"I already can't," he said, straining at the scarves.

I just smiled at him, fluttering my pussy at the tip of his cock, not letting him get more than an inch in. He bucked his hips up, supporting his weight with his feet, but I kept myself away from him, lifting up until I was nearly in the downward-facing dog yoga position. He relaxed again, and I leaned forward to kiss him, putting my weight on his chest, fluttering again.

He lost himself in the kiss, flexing his arms against the restraints, delving into the passion of our locked lips, forgetting for a moment the teasing game I was playing. I didn't forget. The kiss was enough to nearly drive me over the edge.

I chose that moment, when he ceased trying to get deeper, to plunge my hips down on him fully and then sitting back on him with his cock buried to the hilt inside me. I relaxed forward again and fluttered, just giving him that one taste of full impalement.

All this while, my pearls were around my neck, bouncing gently against my chest as I moved, a string of white against my tan skin. I moved down toward Tre, intending to kiss him, but he seized that moment to take the string of pearls in his mouth and hold me there for fear of breaking the strand. While he had me trapped, he thrust into me; he wasn't hard or desperate about it, but slow and intentional, grinning past the pearls in his mouth as he plunged into me.

I almost came, then.

I let him take control, closing back in with him. I had been teasing myself as much as him. I wanted him deep inside me, and depriving myself of that was as titillating for me as it was for him. I was nearing the edge, again, and he was pushing me closer.

He kept his strokes deep and slow, pushing himself as far in as he could go and drawing back out, and I began to match him, pulsing up and back down in time with him.

"Let my arms go," he said. "I want to touch you."

I shook my head. "Make me come first. Then I'll untie you and you can touch me all you want."

I didn't tell him I was close, so close. I was trying to control my reaction, trying to keep my pace steady and stop the whimpers from escaping my lips. I mashed my face into his neck, bit him, unable to stop a gasp from slipping out as he increased his tempo, rocking me harder and harder, and then...oh God, oh my Lord, he slowed it back down, gritting his teeth and gasping into my hair.

"Oh God, Tre, don't stop! Not now! I'm so close, I'm almost there, please...."

He drew himself almost out of me, returning the tease now, just barely brushing my slick, dripping labia with his engorged head. I kept my hips up, holding still, feeling a thrill of lightning shoot through me at each tender, questing touch of his cock. Just when I was about to beg him to finish me, he tilted his hips and slipped back in, moving with an agonizing slowness, millimeter by millimeter.

I broke first. I crushed my pussy down around him, crying out and abandoning all games, all thought. I had come so close to orgasm so many times, been on the cusp of detonation and been brought back away. Now, now with his cock drilling into me, diving with relentless abandon, I came with a fury that erased every orgasm I'd ever had.

In the past, even with Tre, I'd shrieked, whimpered, gasped, cried out, called his name, called on God and heaven and "oh yes fuck me," but never, in all my life, had I ever screamed.

I screamed then, tilting my head back and voicing a full-on scream.

The world went white and I dug my arms around his neck, squeezed with all I had, driving my pussy onto him over and over again, unable to control my body. I saw stars, felt a million galaxies all go supernova in my belly as Tre convulsed into me.

I was still riding the cusp of my orgasm when Tre came, and that sent me over the edge all over again. I felt his penis clench and release, felt the flood his essence fill me, slosh against my walls and drip loose between our joined members. I was sobbing his name into his lips, into his teeth. Our hips were locked together now, moving in sync, both of us orgasming together, and Tre was whispering my name with equal fervor.

"Oh, Shea...oh God, Shea..." his voice was rough with emotion. "Oh my God, that was...I think...I think I just saw heaven."

I lifted my head up enough to meet his eyes. "So did I." I kissed him, a tender caress of the lips. "I'm seeing heaven right now."

I hadn't meant to say that last part, not looking at him the way I was. It was too much like vulnerability, like admitting the truth that was floating around deep inside the core of my soul, behind the walls he was too naive to see.

I wasn't in love with him, but I was close. I could see it happening, if things continued.

That terrified me.

I rolled off of him, untied his wrists from the bed-posts and cuddled into him, pushing down both the fear and the burgeoning attachment with equal ferocity. I tried to hide by not looking at him, knowing he'd see something in my eyes or on my face, and ask about it. He'd ask questions I didn't have the answers to.

"Shea?" His voice was far too concerned and far too full of compassion to ignore.

"Yeah?" I suspected he'd seen or felt what I was hiding.

"What's wrong?"

"Nothing," I lied. "I'm just...spent. I've never in my life felt anything like that before. I don't think I could move if I tried."

"Me either," he said. "But it's more than that. There's something wrong. I can...I don't know, I can feel it. Maybe that sounds crazy, but I can just feel it coming off of you."

I hesitated a beat too long. "It's nothing."

There was anger in his voice when he spoke next. "You're lying to me, Shea." He didn't pull away physically, but I felt him withdrawing emotionally. "I can take it if you want to...be with me. If you—if this is just...just sex, I get that."

He spoke to the ceiling, his arms strong around me, but his heart pulling away. I wasn't sure how it had happened, since we'd done little together but have sex, but somehow I had started feeling something for him besides lust. He was waiting for me to answer, and I couldn't, I just shook my head, and he sighed.

I tried to figure out what had happened. When I saw him in the church, I was immediately attracted to him. He was gorgeous, with his angular face and perfect hair and natural bulk, but it was offset by something in his eyes, a kindness that was genuine, a true, bone-deep

goodness that was truly rare. He was naive, and innocent, though, sheltered from just about everything that
comprises the world at large, life in general. I doubted
he knew how to survive on his own out there, away from
his father. I doubt he understood what love really was,
or how to take care of a woman.

I didn't doubt that he could learn, but my fear was
that I'd have to teach him, and I needed someone that
could not just erase the awful memories of my ex-husband, but to love me like he never did. I wasn't sure I
was ready to try to make that love happen, to let anyone
in. I sure as hell wasn't ready to be a sugar-momma to
a sheltered pastor's kid. The sex was amazing, and we'd
just gotten started, that much was true. I had a feeling
if I stayed with Tre, he'd learn to rock my world in ways
I couldn't even imagine right now, especially if that last
orgasm was anything to judge by.

But was that enough to base a relationship off of? I
knew it wasn't. Dan had done for me what I was doing
for Tre, and I recognized this fact for what it was. Dan
had taken me away from my pigeonhole of a life and
showed me the world. He'd introduced me to sex, to
drinking, to drugs, to gambling and traveling, fine wines
and expensive clothes, five-star hotels and private jets to
secluded island getaways...and through it all, Dan and I
had fucked like rabbits.

It had been just that, though, empty, meaningless
fucking, and now, comparing it to what I had with Tre,

it wasn't even that good. It meant nothing to Dan. I didn't realize that at first, though. I was too young and innocent and honestly blind to the truth to see it. I loved every minute of it, felt worldly and womanly, felt like a seductress, a real Jezebel. Then I started noticing signs of Dan's straying: Lipstick on his collars, come-stains on his boxers that he thought I wouldn't notice, perfume on him I didn't wear. I ignored it, pretended it was fine. That didn't work too long, of course. I eventually caught him in our room, with one hooker sucking his dick, three fingers deep in two more bleach-blond whores. That was the beginning of the end, although it took me a long time to siphon the money I needed.

Tre was silent next to me, not sleeping.

"Tre...I don't even know where to start." I traced the lines of his abs, drifting lower, hoping to distract him; he caught me my hand and pulled it back up. "It's not just sex, I can tell you that much. I don't know what it is, though."

I leaned up on an elbow and looked down at him.

"You want the truth?" He nodded, although I'd meant it rhetorically. "When I first invited you here, I meant it as that...as just sex. I thought you were sexy and I wanted you. I...wanted a distraction. But at some point it started turning into something else. I don't know what, I honestly don't. I care about you. You're a good person, a good man, and I'm so proud of you for standing up to your father. I know how much courage that took."

"Distraction from what?" Tre asked, cutting through to the one thing I'd hoped he miss.

I sighed. "A lot of things."

He took my hand in his, wiggling the diamond ring I still wore. I'd forgotten about that. It wasn't the one Dan had given me; I sold that in New Orleans. It was just a fake hunk of cubic zirconium crap I wore, because married women attracted less attention than a single one. At least, that was the idea. Now I was beginning to think otherwise.

"This?" He said, meaning the ring. "You need distraction from this?"

He thought I was still married, I realized.

"I'm not married, anymore, okay? I left him. That's why I came here, to get away from him."

"So you're divorced?"

"Well, not yet. I had the papers sent to him...to my ex-husband, when I was in Jackson. I have a PO box there. He'll sign and that'll be that."

"If you're not divorced, you're still married." Tre's voice was hard, angry.

"No, Tre, you don't understand. I left him. I don't love him, he doesn't love me. There never was love between us. It was just...a legal marriage. This ring isn't even his, it's fake." I took off the ring and handed to Tre, who examined it in the light of the moon shining through the window. "I just wore it because I thought I'd be accepted more easily if I was married. I didn't come here looking to meet anyone, and then I saw you, and..."

"Marriage is sacred, Shea. I really believe that. I know we did all this, together, but I thought—you said—I don't know...I thought you were divorced. This is adultery."

"Tre, please listen to me." I sat up all the way, and so did he, turning to face me; I took the ring from him and held it between us. "There are two levels to marriage, okay? There's legal marriage, and emotional marriage. You can be one, without being the other. Do you see what I'm saying? Legal marriage is just a formality, invented by men, by people. It's a tax and property thing, and that's it. Emotional marriage, interpersonal marriage...that's different. That's when two people agree that they love each other and that they want to spend their lives together, sharing everything. It's an agreement, a promise, and a...what's the word the bible uses? A covenant. It's not a legal thing.

"So technically, legally, yes, I'm still married, and this would be adultery in that sense. But in the kind of marriage I believe the Bible means when it talks about adultery...no, I don't believe that's what we're doing."

Tre looked away, staring out the window. He rubbed his temples and got up from the bed, pacing naked over to the window. He was silent a long time, thinking. I gave him the space. It felt like a trivial justification, what I'd just given him, and I think he knew it.

"I don't know, Shea. That seems like an excuse. I mean, I get what you're saying about two kinds of marriage, and I agree, now that I think about it. But I can't help wondering...is it still wrong, even if it's just legal marriage, that doesn't mean anything to either you or your husband, ex-husband, or whatever? And if it's not cheap, meaningless sex, what is it? It's sex outside of marriage, for one thing, and that's still a sin."

"Is it? Where does it say that? Where does it say sex is wrong?"

Tre stopped and thought, then waved his hand in a dismissal. "You're justifying. I know what I said earlier, that I didn't care if it was wrong, but now I do."

I set the ring down on the bedside table and crossed the room to stand next to him. I didn't touch him, though. I didn't want to seduce him out of his beliefs. Not entirely, at least.

"Tre, you have to decide what you believe for yourself. I think you're still partially thinking with the beliefs your father drilled into you. What do you believe, for yourself? Do you think what we have is wrong?"

"What do we have, Shea? You said yourself you don't know what it is. I mean, where is this going? How long are we going to continue this? It's wonderful, and amazing, and I...God, I don't want to stop. But is it wrong? I don't know. I'm so confused, suddenly. I like you. I really, really like you. Too much, maybe. My heart goes all weird when I think about you. That sounded stupid, I'm sorry." Tre turned to look at me, gilded silver by the moonlight. "Am I falling in love with you? I barely know you. I don't...I mean, we've known each other for like, three days. Two, actually. And we've spent most of that making love. Do I just think I feel this way because of that? Because of the sex? I don't know."

"Here's the thing. Only you can decide what you feel. I like spending time with you, being with you, and I hope you decide to stay with me, but I'm not going to try to influence your beliefs or feelings beyond that. If I did, I'd be no better than your father."

Tre turned back to the window, and I could see the conflict written in the lines of his face, the set of his mouth, the tension of his shoulders. He seemed suddenly very much a man, rather than the awkward, hesitant not-quite-a-man he'd been just a few days ago.

"I can't go back," he said, after a while. "I can't go back to being who I was. Maybe it's not being a virgin anymore, maybe its knowing my parents—my dad— don't love me anymore, but everything just seems... different. It's like...it's like being with you, having sex or making love or whatever you want to call it, changed the way I see the world, or...the way I see myself, and life, and God, and...just everything."

"It'll do that," I said. "I know what you're going through, to an extent. My ex-husband, Dan, I ran away with him when I was sixteen, almost seventeen. I remember suddenly looking at everyone around me with new eyes, sexual eyes, adult eyes. Even if you don't feel desire for them, you see them differently, knowing they've done what you've done, and it does change the way you see, the way you think and feel."

I wrapped my arms around his waist; he held himself stiff for a moment, then softened and turned to hold me, pulling me against his chest. My head nestled in the hollow beneath his chin, fitting as if formed to rest there.

"Do you resent me for taking your innocence?" I asked.

That was a question, a fear, that had been lurking in my heart for a while now. I waited for his answer with a pounding heart and suddenly tear-burnt eyes. This tryst was turning intense, morphing out of my control into something frighteningly like a relationship.

"No," came the answer, whispered into my hair. "I made the choice. I came here, knowing, at least in some way, what you wanted, and I wanted it too. When I stepped into this house, I knew I was crossing some kind of line that I wouldn't be able to uncross. I did it anyway, and that was my choice, Shea. You didn't take my innocence; I gave it to you. I don't regret it.

"I just don't know where we go from here." This last part was whispered more to himself than to me, and I didn't respond.

I didn't know either.

Five

My Audi's engine hummed, purring smoothly as Tre guided my car around the gentle curve of the highway. The top was down, wind whipping our hair, the sun warming us as we cruised south on US-49 towards Jackson.

Tre had decided upon waking the next morning to make a clean break.

"I want to leave," he had said at breakfast.

"Leave? Okay. Where do you want to go, and for how long?"

He met my eyes, and his were intense, determined. "I mean, leave Jackson. Move away, permanently."

I was shocked. "Okay...um...okay. Are you sure?"

He nodded. "I'm not just assuming we'll stay together, if you're not ready for that. I don't want to assume that this is...something it may not be, for you."

I took a moment, thinking. I looked around me, out the sliding glass door to the yard I'd never been in. I realized there was nothing here for me. If Tre left, I'd leave.

"Alright," I said. "Let's go then. Let's go now. I'll pack a bag and we can go."

He drove to his parents' house in his old F-150, his duffel in the trunk of my car. This time I went in with him, dressed somewhat conservatively in a pair of jeans and a not-too-revealing T-shirt. I held Tre's hand as we stood in the foyer of his parent's house, matching stares with his father. His mother sat in a La-Z-boy, cross-stitching a simple pattern into a cloth stretched across a round hoop. She didn't look up when Tre entered, didn't give him a greeting, or even acknowledge his presence.

"What do you want?" Tre's father said. "And why have you brought this prostitute into my house?"

Tre's eyes narrowed, his jaw clenched, and his fingers curled into a fist. Before I could stop him, Tre had let go of my hand, took three long steps, and floored his father with a thunderous right hook. Pastor McNabb tumbled backward, fell to his backside, his nose gushing blood, broken.

"She's not a prostitute, Dad," Tre said past clenched teeth. "And we came to say goodbye. I'm leaving. Permanently. I know better than to think you'd ever change your mind about me, or Shea."

Tre's mother had glanced up now, weak brown eyes wide, hands stilled on her cross-stitching hoop, needle pinched between trembling fingers. His father remained on the floor, letting his nose bleed onto his white button-down.

Tre waited, but neither of his parents said anything. "Fine, don't say nothin'. You're my parents, and I love you. At least, I want to. But if you're so closed-minded as to disown me over this, without talking to me about it, or knowing a damn thing about Shea...then I guess it's just as well. You'd have never accepted me anyway, not if I didn't live my life your way." Tre turned and stalked to the door, face expressionless and hard, and took my hand; he spoke without turning around. "So... goodbye. I hope this is worth it to you, 'cause you ain't never gonna see me again."

Tre's mother took a deep breath, mouth trembling, cross-stitching wavering in her hand. She stood up, reached for Tre with a thin-fingered, gnarl-knuckled hand, as if to stop him. Then, with a single glance at her cowering, bleeding husband, she lowered her head and sat back down. I watched in a kind of apathetic horror as she took the needle in now-calm fingers and plunged it into the white fabric and threaded it back through. She didn't look up again, didn't move to help her bleeding husband. She never spoke a word.

Tre's father, Pastor Brian McNabb, stood as Tre walked out, me trailing behind him by the hand. I stopped, and Tre jerked his hand free and continued to my car.

"You're a fool, Pastor," I said. "Tre is a good man. Mark my words: you'll regret this, someday. You'll realize what you lost and you'll want him back, but he'll be gone."

I turned away then, too, and returned to my car. Tre had left the keys to his truck in the ignition, as the vehicle had been a gift from his parents.

His duffel bag had about a month's worth of clothes, some toiletries, and a worn Bible, dog-eared black leather with gold-edged pages and his name inscribed in the bottom corner: Timothy Robert Evan McNabb. He brought nothing else. No pictures, no cell phone, no memorabilia of his life in Yazoo City. Just some practical necessities and a Bible.

Tre was sitting in the passenger seat, staring ahead, hands on his thighs. The only trace of emotion was the pulsing of a vein in his temple, a single throbbing string of purple.

I slid into the driver's seat, pushed the shifter into first, then hesitated, not releasing the clutch yet.

"Tre, are you sure—"

"Just drive."

I nodded and pulled away slowly, heading towards the highway.

"Can you stop by Jimmy's? I want to say good-bye." Tre spoke without looking at me, still motionless, appearing calm.

I could tell he was seething inside, hiding a maelstrom of emotions beneath a forced façade of calm. I headed towards his friend's house. I tried to take his hand, but he pulled his away.

"I need some time, Shea," he said. "I'm sorry. I'm too pissed off right now."

I just nodded and drove in silence.

Jimmy watched us coming from his porch, hands shoved into his pockets. Tre got out of the car and ascended the porch steps to shake Jimmy's hand; I stayed in the car. The two men didn't speak for a few minutes, just trading the look of friends of who don't need words to communicate.

"I hit him, Jimmy. I broke his nose and knocked him onto his ass."

Jimmy nodded. "He had it coming, I guess."

Tre looked at the back of his hand, the one he'd punched his father with, as if it had the answers to life's questions. "I'm leavin', Jimmy. I ain't comin' back, neither."

Tre's accent was thick suddenly, and I knew he was trying to contain his emotions.

Jimmy just nodded again. "I figured you would, someday. 'Specially after you met her," he said, jerking a thumb at me. "She's good for you. You're too special for a place like this, I've always known that. I'll sure miss you, buddy, but you can't stay here. I know that. Now go on, get outta here. Write me a letter or somethin', will you?"

Tre nodded, hesitated, then pulled Jimmy into a hug. They hugged like men, slapping backs, a good foot between them, heads held stiff, sideways.

"I'll see you, Jimmy," Tre said, stepping away and down the four thumping wooden steps.

"No you won't," Jimmy said.

He reached into his back pocket and pulled out a folding knife and tossed it to Tre, who caught it, looked at it, and glanced up at Jimmy, shock in his eyes.

"You sure? This is—"

"I know. Yeah, I figure if you ain't coming back, you'd best have somethin' to remember me by."

Tre nodded, held up the knife in a salute, and slid into the car, nodding at me to drive. I backed out onto the packed-dirt county road, and Tre waved once before we pulled out of sight. He stared down at the knife Jimmy had given him. It was a hunter's folding blade, long and wide, made of antler and stainless steel. It looked old, battered and worn and well-cared for.

"It was his great-grandfather's," Tre said, after several miles of silence. "He meant to give it to his kid, if he ever got married."

He opened it, ran his thumb across the blade's edge, nodded once, and closed it, put it in his hip pocket.

We made it to US-49 before his emotions got free. It started with a shake of the head, as if to brush away a buzzing fly, then a dash of his wrist across his cheek. I glanced at him, but he turned away to watch the cotton rows flit past, hiding from me. His shoulders started to shake, and he pressed the heels of his hands into his eye sockets, like he could push the tears back in with brute force.

I pulled over to the shoulder, took his hand in mine, tangled our fingers together. He tried to pull away, and I could feel his sense of shame keeping him turned away from me.

I held his hand, and said, "It's okay to be upset, Tre. You're leaving everything you know. I don't think less of you for crying. You'll still be a man if you cry a little."

He ventured a look at me, eyes red, brimming. I smiled at him, kissed him, tasting tears. He shuddered, trembled against my lips, and then broke down. I unbuckled my seat belt and pulled him against me, let him get it out. After a few minutes, he sniffed hard, rubbed his eyes and got out of the car, striding into the cotton field. I let him walk. He came back and I got out, put the top down, and pulled him into another embrace, but this time I pressed my body against him, kissed him hard.

He returned the kiss, moving against me, holding me tight. We pulled apart after a minute, ignoring the honks of passing cars, and Tre moved to get back in the passenger seat.

"Why don't you drive?" I said.

He nodded, smiling. I don't think he'd ever driven a vehicle other than the truck. He slid in, adjusted the seat and the mirrors, put it in first, and promptly stalled out.

I laughed. "It's a tighter clutch than your truck. You have to punch it a little."

He nodded, started the car and tried again, this time he punched the gas, rocketing the powerful little car forward along the shoulder until he had enough speed to match the flow of traffic.

We drove in a companionable silence, Tre lost in his thoughts, me in mine. After about half an hour, traffic thinned out. My hand was on Tre's leg, and I moved it toward his crotch, rubbing the seam of his jeans. He looked at me, a questioning half-smile on his lips.

"Just drive," I told him, grinning a promise at him. "Put it in cruise control."

He did as I told him, and kept his eyes on the road, glancing at me once then back to the road.

I rubbed at him, feeling him thicken under his jeans, pushing against the fabric. We were cruising along an empty highway now, and I unzipped his jeans, unbuttoned them, and reached my fingers between the gap of his boxers. His cock was semi-rigid, firming up in my hand as I slipped my palm up and down his growing length. I unbuckled, leaned across and licked him, tonguing the head, tasting his pre-come as it oozed from the tiny hole. I ran my mouth sideways along him, moistening him, rubbing my thumb in circles around his head. He kept his hands clenched on the wheel, struggling to hold his hips still.

He was rock-hard now, and I used my saliva on his cock as lubrication, pumping my fist around his cock, licking the tip, sucking it. When he started to groan and move his hips despite his attempts at control, I took him all the way in my mouth and dipped my head up and down on him, still pumping with one hand.

"I'm...I'm gonna..." Tre gasped, wrapping his fingers in my hair, "Oh, God...I'm coming..."

I felt his cock tighten and then salty, liquid heat hit the back of my throat. I sucked hard, still moving my hand on him; he whimpered in the back of his throat, moving his hips in small thrusts as I lifted my head free. He glanced down at me, and I gave his cock a long, intentional swipe with my tongue, meeting his eyes.

I tucked him back in, zipped him and buttoned him, re-buckling. A car zipped past us just as I sat up, and the man driving gave Tre a knowing grin. The woman just rolled her eyes and shook her head. Tre seemed mortified that they'd correctly assumed what had just happened.

"Do you know them?" I asked.

"No."

"Then why are you worried about what they think? The guy was jealous, I can tell you that much." I laughed. "I bet she's probably not ever given him road-head. She probably doesn't go down on him at all."

Tre tilted his head. "No? Why not?"

I laughed again, realizing this was something else he just didn't have any way of knowing. "Well, sex is like anything else, honey. Not everyone is the same. Some women like giving head, some don't. Some will do it if they're asked to, some won't, and others would rip you a new one for even suggesting it. It's just a personal thing."

"I can't imagine asking you to do that," Tre said. "I mean, I like it a lot, but it seems like something that would have to be your choice."

"That's sweet, Tre, and I wouldn't expect anything different from a guy like you. And that's why I'll keep doing it to you."

"What's that mean? A guy like me?"

"Well, just that you're considerate, and generous. and kind. You think about me, as well as yourself, if not more."

"Well, yeah," Tre said, sounding as if such a thing was obvious.

"Not everyone is like that. It's rare, actually. Most guys don't care about what their partner wants or feels. Sex is about getting them off and that's it."

Tre shrugged. "I guess I was just raised to think about other people. My dad may have been a bad father in some ways, but he did instill some values in me that I think are good things."

I squeezed his hand. "I agree. I think someday your father is going to regret driving you away."

"I don't want to think about him anymore," Tre said.

Silence, then, for several miles.

"Shea? You've...you've done all this before, haven't you? Sex, I mean."

"Tre..." I sighed. "Yeah, I have. Do you really need to ask?"

He shrugged. "Well, I knew, since you were married, and older than me and whatever...I knew you had, and you act like you know what you're doing. I just...I don't like thinking about you with anyone else. I know you don't belong to me or anything, it just—"

"Tre, listen. Yeah, I've done all this before. I know what I'm doing from experience. I'll tell you whatever you want to know about me, but, in my experience, there are some things better left unasked. I'm not keeping secrets from you, please understand that. If you ask me a question, I'll tell the truth. But, please think about it before asking, because once you know, you can't un-know it."

"Were there others besides your ex-husband?"

"A couple, right after I left him. Just quick, one-night things that didn't mean anything and didn't even feel that great. Before you, it had been a while. More than a year, in fact."

Tre nodded. "Why'd you leave him?"

"That's a long, long story, Tre, and not a pretty one."

"We have time."

So I told him. Tre listened intently, not interrupting as I talked about Dan sweeping me away from sleepy old Savannah, going from being a poor country pastor's daughter to being the wife of a wealthy casino magnate, learning about the world and sex and money. Learning about unfaithfulness, and the difference between sex and love. Learning the hard, painful way that Dan expected me to ignore his cheating, but refused to tolerate mine.

We pulled into Jackson as I finished my story.

"Thanks for telling me, Shea," Tre said.

"So...what do you think about me now?" I asked.

He thought before answering. "Well. I think you were just a girl when he took you. I know you went with him, but I don't think you were in any position to make that choice properly. I think you did the best you could, and I think I'm glad you left him." He was silent for a moment, then glanced at me as we stopped at a traffic light.

"Will he come after you?"

I turned to watch the buildings pass by. "No, I don't think so. I left him almost two years ago, and I haven't heard a word from him. He's got the resources to find me, if he wanted to. He's the kind of guy who can afford to pay what it takes to find a person, wherever they are."

"What if he does?"

I sighed. "Let's not borrow trouble, Tre."

I directed him to a hotel and we checked in, and Tre carried his duffel and my little suitcase. I'd only brought a few necessities. I planned to have a moving company pack everything up for me later. We showered separately, and I told Tre to dress nice, as I wanted to go on a date with him. All our time thus far had been spent in bed or at my house. I wanted to take him out, parade him on my arm, show him the big city.

I took him to Nick's in Fondren, and we spent a long evening drinking wine, eating, and talking. I was discovering that what Tre lacked in urban sophistication, he more than made up for in curiosity, eagerness to learn, and a capacity for stimulating conversation.

I found myself staring at him as we talked, watching his black-shadowed chin move, watching his eyes like cinnamon-sprinkled cocoa move with restless energy, his thick, gentle fingers always tapping the table or twisting a napkin or playing with his fork. His ink-dark hair constantly fell across his left eye, and he brushed it aside with a thumb. He was wearing a short sleeve blue button-down that left his biceps almost bare, stretching across his broad chest. He'd buttoned it almost to the collar, but before we left I undid the second button, exposing a portion of his smooth chest.

I had been attracted to Dan, of course. He was the epitome of polished charm, calculated swagger, and sleek, expensive manners. I was, then, just an unfinished corn-fed country girl, decked out in cut-off jean shorts that Daddy wouldn't have approved of, but he was dead so I wore them to spite him for leaving me. Dan drove through Savannah, saw me lounging on a park bench, reading a book, and he proceeded to charm the pants off me, literally. He talked me into his hotel room, got me hot and bothered with well-placed hands and lips, convinced me to let him touch me, got my hands curious with his seductive words and then it was too late, he was already there, poking me with a sharp pinch and slow movements that started to feel good, after the initial pain. After that, it was easy to believe his cool promises and to be impressed by his Jaguar and his Rolex and his easy talk of million-dollar condos. I left Savannah in his Jag without so much as a note to my mother or sisters.

Tre...oh, Tre was different, as opposite as it was possible to be. He wasn't at all polished, and he was unsophisticated in the ways of city life. He stared at the buildings and the people, fascinated by a place as tiny and backwater as Jackson. I imagined him in New York, or Paris, or Beijing, or Johannesburg, and I smiled at the idea. He was so genuine, though, his inherent kindness shone through in everything he did. He was prone to thinking before he answered, and his responses were always well-phrased and articulate. His father, for all his hard-headed, hard-right morality, was an intelligent, educated man who had passed this quality on to his son. There was ruggedness to Tre, though, a wildness to him.

He would be at home on a horse, or a hiking trail. He had shown a dangerous side, too, when he punched his father, who wasn't a small man by any means. I thought again, as we walked along the Pearl River, that Tre was wasted in a place like Yazoo City.

We were heading back to our hotel, passing by a narrow alley, the hour late, the city dark and quiet. A young man jumped out at us, wielding a long, wicked knife. He was maybe eighteen, white, his dirty, ragged, appearance, track-scarred arms and rail-thin, gaunt frame proclaiming him a drug addict. He jabbed the knife at me, threatening rather than attacking.

"Give me money," he said, showing yellow, rotting teeth. "Gimme all your money, or I'll kill her."

Tre shifted subtly in front of me, and I willingly moved behind him.

"Why don't you put the knife down and we'll talk," Tre said, holding his hands in front of him.

He sounded calm, but I could see the tension and fear in the curl of his shoulders, the coiled-spring way he stood.

"Shut the fuck up!" Fear, desperation, and raw hunger blazed in the addict's eyes. "Shut up! Money, or you die!"

"Listen, we'll help you," Tre said, taking a slow step forward. "Just put the knife away. We'll get you help. You're sick. You don't need to threaten us."

It happened like a nightmare lightning strike. The dirty young man lashed out with his knife, jabbing forward with the blade up. Tre knocked the blade aside, taking a long, deep cut along the outside of his forearm. He latched onto the knife-arm with his unwounded hand, clamping down with all his strength, twisting the arm upside down and putting his weight onto the stressed joint. The addict screamed, shrill and panicked.

Tre glared into the young man's eyes, and I saw the anger, the pent-up rage burning there, fueled by adrenaline. Tre's fist lifted up, cocked back, lashed out and connected with the other man's jaw. Teeth crumbled and fell loose, accompanied by blood and drool. The knife clattered to the ground, and Tre kicked it away, stepping back from the addict, who was clutching his mouth and moaning.

Tre pulled me away, turning his back on our attacker. I was opening my mouth to warn him when I caught a glimpse of motion from the corner of my eye. I shoved Tre, feeling a cold bite of pain along my shoulder. Tre bounced off the wall, grappled with the addict, who was strengthened now by pain and desperation. Tre was pressed back against the alley wall, the knife closing in on his face, holding it away with one hand, the other bleeding and scrabbling at his opponent's face.

The tableau froze like that for a second that stretched into eternity, and then snapped in a rush. Tre's fingers clamped onto the addict's throat, squeezing his windpipe, crushing it with inexorable fingers. A twist of his body, and Tre was shoving the attacker away, bashing out with a fist like a jackhammer, pounding, pounding, pounding. He was holding the bloody young man's frame up with one hand and bashing with the other, smashing mercilessly.

I found my senses, called Tre's name and touched his shoulder. "It's over, Tre! Let go! Stop!" I pulled him away, pushed him back from the limp form. "Come on, Tre, it's fine. He's down, you won."

Tre shook his head as if to clear it of a fog. He started, looking at the unconscious body at his feet.

"Is he...did I...?"

I knelt down by the body, listening. There was a gasping, gurgling breath, a low, weak moan.

"No, he's alive," I said.

I pulled out my cell phone and dialed 911. The next several hours passed in stretching-toffee blur. We answered questions, got attended by paramedics, who put a bandage on the shallow cut on my shoulder, announcing that Tre needed stitches. The police filed their reports, telling us not to leave Jackson, but that it was unlikely Tre would be charged with anything, as the young man who'd attacked us was wanted in connection with several other muggings. He'd stabbed several people, actually, killing one and wounding the rest.

We went to the hospital, where we sat waiting in silence for an interminable number of hours, time without passage, just a ticking clock, a hard plastic hospital seat and the mobile bed. Eventually the hospital people came, nurses and anesthetists and the doctor, and his arm was stitched up, twenty sutures along his forearm.

It was nearly dawn by the time we got back to our hotel room, and we collapsed into bed, exhausted. I woke with mid-afternoon sun shining on me, snugged against Tre's chest. I let myself wake up slowly, savoring the peace, the muzzy warmth and Tre's skin against my face. After a while I slipped out of bed and took a long shower. When I emerged wrapped in a towel, steam billowing around me, Tre was awake.

"How are you feeling?" I asked.

"Like I could use a shower," he said. "But fine, otherwise."

"All yours, then," I said.

He didn't move, though. His eyes were on me, watching me, so I dropped the towel and did my hair with the bathroom door open, naked. I left my face make-up free, since I anticipated it getting smudged in the near future. After I finished brushing my teeth, he got in the shower, and I lay on the bed, watching him through the open door. I felt lust for his body pool in my belly and spread to my thighs. He toweled off, brushed his teeth, oblivious to my gaze. He came out, the towel wrapped around his waist, low and showing that V, that delicious arrowhead leading to his manhood.

I was naked on the bed, waiting for him. I lay on my side, supporting my head on my hand. He approached the bed slowly, and the towel around him began to bulge outward. He crossed around to the side of the bed, facing me, looking down at me with desire blazing in his eyes. I kept still, willing him to make the first move. His hands twitched at his sides, then reached for me, and I forced myself to hold still yet longer, even though I desperately wanted to roll over onto my back and pull him down to me and feel his hands on me, devour me, plunder me.

He leaned down, kissed me, one hand propping him up on the bed, the other roving from my hip, caressing my ass with a brief graze before moving up my side, tickling my ribs. He cupped my breast and thumbed my aching, stiffened nipples, learning now how I liked to be touched. I moaned into his mouth when his fingers traced down from my breast to my pussy and nudged at me. I lifted my leg aside, granting him access to my opening, and he inserted a gentle pair of fingers into me. I let my hand tug aside the towel and grasp his hardening member as it sprang free, moaning again at the feel of him in my hand, anticipating his entrance into me, huge and hard and so thorough, so satisfying.

He moved to get on the bed, but I stopped him. "I want you to take me from behind," I told him.

"From behind? Like, in the..."

I shook my head and stood up, kissing him, fondling his cock as I dipped my tongue into his mouth.

"No, not there, not yet," I said. "I'll show you."

I turned around and bent over the bed, snagging a pillow and stuffing it under my stomach to lift me up farther. Tre pressed himself against me, and my eyes fluttered at the pressure of his hot length against the seam of my ass, his probing tip pressing against my anus. I considered, briefly, putting him in that opening, but decided to leave that for another time. Neither of us was ready for that, just yet. I reached behind me and guided him down to my pussy, lifting up on my toes and sinking down onto him as he thrust himself in.

I gasped, full of him, wet and ready for him. He moaned, pulsing into me, slowly at first, experimental thrusts. I moved my hips against him, encouraging him. I called his name, breathless already. He started to push harder, and then he leaned into me, taking my grinding hips in his hands and jerking me into him.

He slowed, suddenly.

"No!" I said. "Don't stop, please!"

"I'm already there," he gasped, "I want you to... come with me."

I pushed my ass down against him, starting my own rhythm. "I will, I will, I promise," I said. "I want to feel you come, I want to feel you lose it, deep inside me."

He started to move again, pushing into me, and the brief pause had brought him back from the edge. He thrust, thrust, thrust, harder now, his hands pulling me with increasing violence into him, a near-savagery that shocked me.

"Yes, yes, Tre! Fuck me so hard," I said, with a gasp and a whimper, "I love it like this, give it to me hard!"

Tre complied, moving harder until he was slamming his cock into me, stabbing deep, pushing into the very uttermost depths of my pussy, drawing ecstasy from me with each push. He came hard, blasting his seed into me, groaning and crying my name, "Shea, Shea, yes, Shea!"

His hands were rough and strong on my hips, pulling me into him as he came. My orgasm began as he buried himself with slow, hard thrusts into me, and I clawed the pillow as small explosions rocked through me.

"Don't stop, don't stop!" I said, shoving my buttocks into him furiously, gasping his name now in the rhythm of his thrusts into me.

I came with explosive fury, and he felt it, caught the intensity of it and redoubled his frenzied ramming into me, even though he was already done and his come dripping out of me now. He kept going, kept going, softening but still filling me, driving the orgasm to an agonizing roar of rapturous delight through me, until I was sobbing and limp, my folds sore from his passion, throbbing with pulsating pleasure.

He picked me up in his arms, and easily lifted me to the bed, gathered me against him, suddenly as tender as he had been savage a moment ago. Our breathing matched, quick, heaving gasps, as we lay together sweat-slick and spent.

When I could breathe, I said, "Oh my good Lord, Tre...I have never in my life been fucked that hard."

"I didn't hurt you did I?" Tre said, apprehensive now.

"It's a good hurt, baby," I said. "I loved it. I love making you lose control on me. You'd never hurt me on purpose, I know that."

"I did hurt you, though." It wasn't a question.

"I'll be a bit tender for a few minutes, yes. You were very...passionate."

He looked at me across the pillow, his eyes sorrowful and apologetic. "I'm so sorry, Shea, I shouldn't have...I don't know what came over me, I just...something about that position, I felt you and I just...I lost it. I didn't mean to hurt you, I'm so, so sorry."

I rolled over on top of him, took his face in my hands. His tenderness and abject pain at the thought of having hurt me was too much, too deep. It pierced my heart, pulled down more of the walls I'd been trying to put up between my inner soul and the feelings that were developing for Tre.

"Listen to me, baby," I said, letting the affectionate name drop with intentional emphasis.

"You didn't hurt me, okay? Not like you're thinking. I'm completely fine. You were wonderful, so, so wonderful. I would have stopped you if you were actually hurting me. I promise. I loved it. Do you hear me? I wanted you to lose control. I wanted it hard. Did you hear me telling you to give it to me? I was saying that because it felt good, so, so good."

Tre searched my eyes, looking for the lie, for the covering up of his feelings, or the hint that would tell him I was just trying to pacify him. I held his rough cheeks in my hands and let him look, tried to put everything into my gaze. I let the conflict, the burgeoning love... yes, love...the fear, all of it.

At length he lay back down, satisfied with what he saw.

"Baby?" he asked, between the spaces of our synchronized heart beats.

I nodded. "Baby. Honey. Sweetie." I tilted my head to look up at him across his chest. "I can think of others."

"Baby. No one has ever called me that."

"You were wonderful, baby. Thank you" I said it as tenderly as I could.

His chest swelled with a long breath, and imagined the inbreath was the swelling of my love expanding into him. I was terrified of loving him, terrified more still that he would love me back. I knew he did, which is why it scared me. We were in uncharted waters for both of us. I didn't know how to love any more than he did. I had never loved Dan, nor been loved by him.

"I still don't know what came over me, why I went crazy like that."

"I do."

He cocked an eyebrow at me. "You do?"

"Well, it was two things. One, the adrenaline from last night, the rush of testosterone and all that. You went warrior on that guy, protecting your lady—which was hot, by the way. Seeing you fight to protect me, it was scary then, but thinking about it now gets me wet for you all over again. And number two, I think you just really like taking me from behind."

"It did feel incredible," he said.

"Good," I said. "I'll give it to you like that whenever you want. I like it too."

More silence, and then his voice, tense: "I really messed that guy up."

I thought for a moment, trying to formulate the best response. "You were protecting me, and yourself. He would have killed one or both of us. You did what you had to." I rubbed my hands on his chest as I spoke. "The police didn't seem to think you were at fault either, so that has to tell you something."

"True," he said. "It was just scary. I saw him lunge at you, saw the knife cut you, and I went berserk."

"I know. It's okay. It's an instinct." I let my hand roam south along his torso, cupping his testicles, feeling them tighten in response to my touch; he would be ready again soon, and so would I. "And like I said, it turns me on. A woman likes to feel safe, and now I know you can and will protect me."

He smiled at me, rolling over to kiss me. It was a long, slow, tender kiss, full of the new spikes of love between us. This time, instead of blossoming immediately into lustful twisting and rubbing, we let the kiss go, let it curl around us and through us, merging our hearts and souls in a way no sexual act ever could. I felt his arms around me, and the knowledge that he was willing to risk death to protect me gave wings to my new-found love for Tre.

I don't know how long we kissed, how long we delved into each other; it could have been five minutes, or it could have been five hours. All I know is at some point, without either of us instigating it, Tre was on top of me, moving inside me with exquisite gentility, eyes boring into me, questioning. I was still a little sore, but he was gentle, and I felt nothing but the pleasure of his love, the heart-cracking wellspring of emotion in his eyes, in the slow, delicious strokes of him inside me. There was no weight against me, just him gliding deep and pulling back, just his lips against mine, against my breasts, our stomachs touching, brushing. This time, we came at the same moment, a long rolling ocean of pleasure, our breaths hitching into sobs, our hearts tangled and merged.

We slept again, deep and without dreams, wrapped in each other, content in a soul-deep way.

For the second time since I first slept with Tre, I was woken by the sound of angry pounding on the door.

There was no furious shouting, though, and some primal instinct clamped around my heart.

"Will you answer that, Tre?" I asked, fear make my voice tiny.

He didn't answer, just stood up, wrapped a towel around his hips, and strode confidently to the door, fists curled at his sides. I clutched the sheet to my chest, terrified of who I knew was on the other side of the door.

Tre blocked my view, but I heard the angry, familiar voice. "Who the hell are you? Where's Shea?"

Tre's voice was cold, hard, and threatening. "What do you want?"

"I want my wife!"

I saw Tre flinch, then straighten and step forward, pushing Dan backwards. "Shea isn't your wife anymore, Dan. She doesn't belong to you. Leave now."

I heard then the unmistakable sound of a pistol's slide being drawn back.

"She'll always belong to me."

Six

My heart stopped, and my mouth went dry. Tre tensed, but held his position.

"She's a woman, Dan," Tre said, "not a possession. Go away."

Tre stumbled backward with Dan following, the barrel of a pistol pressed against Tre's forehead.

"Don't tell me what to do, you little shit," Dan said, shoving the gun to send Tre stumbling backward. "I'll fucking kill you and no one will give a fuck."

Dan's pale blue eyes found me, a greedy, lecherous smile curved his mouth. "I see you got the whore all ready for me." He gestured with the barrel of the gun. "Get over here, bitch."

Tre's eyes were blazing with anger and fear. He glanced at me, and I shook my head. I didn't want him to get hurt because of me. I slid off the bed, keeping the sheet wrapped around my chest.

"Lose the sheet, Shea." Dan tilted the gun toward his crotch, and then pointed it at Tre. "Get on your knees and blow me, or I'll blast the punk's head off."

I swallowed hard, my hands shaking. I didn't want to do this, but I couldn't let Tre get hurt.

"No, Shea, don't," Tre said, his voice strained. I didn't dare look at him. "Don't do it."

Dan glanced at Tre, contemptuous. Dan was shorter than Tre by several inches, thinner and had nowhere near the same bulk. He was dressed in an expensive suit, wore a Rolex and snakeskin shoes, gaudy gold rings on his fingers. His fine blond hair was coming loose at the sides, slicked back on the top. Dan was tense, nervous, fidgety, angry.

Tre, on the other hand, was naked except for the towel cinched around his waist. Fear and anger showed in Tre's dark brown eyes, but he was leaning back against the wall, arms crossed, seemingly relaxed. He was ready to pounce, I could tell. He had no intention of letting this happen.

I was frozen. I didn't know what to do. There was no way I could touch Dan. I'd rather die first. The problem was, Dan would kill Tre instead of me.

Dan pulled back the hammer of the pistol. "Now, bitch."

I forced my feet forward, one step at a time, still clutching the sheet to my chest. A few, far-too-short steps took me within hand's grasp of Dan. He snatched the sheet from my stiffened fingers, and I was naked, vulnerable. Dan reached for me again, with the hand gripping the pistol, pushed my head down. His other hand moved for his zipper, lowered it. He rooted in his boxers and pulled out his penis, still trying to force my unwilling head down.

For that split second, Tre was forgotten, all of Dan's attention focused on bending me to his will.

Out of the corner of my eye, I saw a flash of movement, tan skin rippling through space. I threw myself to the side as Tre collided with Dan in a bone-crunching tackle. The gun went flying, landed under a chair. Tre and Dan rolled and came to a stop with Tre on top, fists flying, bashing, smashing. Dan's face crumpled under Tre's fist, and once again I had to pull him away. Tre scrambled away from the prone, limp, and bleeding form of my husband. My ex-husband. He may not have signed the papers, but he wasn't my husband.

Tre scooped up his jeans and shoved his legs into them, then stripped the bed of its sheets. He rummaged through Dan's pockets, emptying them, then manhandled his body into a chair, using the bed sheets to tie him up.

I was still frozen, shocked.

"Get dressed, Shea," Tre ordered. I stared at him, uncomprehending. "Shea? Are you with me? I ain't stayin' here. We gotta go. Come on, baby. Get dressed."

"Go? Where are we going?"

"Anywhere. Away from here, away from him." He grabbed my bra from the handle of the bathroom door where I'd left it, handed it to me, then pulled a clean pair of panties from my suitcase, along with a pair of boy-shorts and a T-shirt.

I put them on, numb. Seeing Dan had thrown my brain out of gear and I couldn't seem to get it to click back into place. Having clothes on got me running a bit better. I packed the rest of our stuff, and then Tre grabbed our bags as well as the set of keys from Dan's pockets. The key was for an Aston Martin.

Tre vanished out the door with our things, leaving me alone with Dan, who was beginning to stir. Blood drooled from his jaw, congealed at his nose and covered his neck and shirt front. His bruised, purpling eyes fluttered, and then he jerked awake, struggled against the sheets binding him. They held tight. I scooped the gun up from beneath the chair.

Blind hate flooded through me, now, with Dan bound helpless in front of me. I could get revenge. I pressed the pistol to his head, remembering all the insults, the times he'd slapped me, the hookers, the drugs...

"Do it," Dan slurred. "Shoot me. You know you want to."

I did want to. It would be so easy. I pulled the hammer back with both thumbs, shoved the barrel into his mouth.

Then I felt firm hands pull the gun away from me, felt Tre's hands twist me aside.

"No, Shea. Let's just go. Leave him." Tre guided me to the door and pushed me through it. I heard him do something behind me, then a thump of the gun hitting the floor and Tre's hand touched me on the back.

"What did you do?" I asked.

"Wiped prints off it. I saw an episode of CSI, once, while my folks were out."

He helped me into a car, tan leather seats. Tre slipped in beside me in the driver's seat, started the car with a smooth purr. It wasn't my car, it was Dan's. The Aston Martin. His baby. His pride and joy. I grinned. Having this car stolen would really chap his ass.

Tre drove fast, enjoying the power of the car.

"Slow down, Tre," I said, shock finally wearing off. "This is a stolen car, after all."

"True." He brought the car down to a safe, legal speed.

We drove south in silence for a few miles. After a while, Tre finally glanced at me. He was antsy in the driver's seat, tapping his fingers, eyes flicking. I wasn't sure if he was nervous from having stolen a three hundred thousand dollar car, or if he was flushed with adrenaline from the fight. Both, most likely

"Are you okay?" He asked.

"It was scary. Seeing him...it threw me for a loop. I don't know why he finally showed up after all this time." I tried a smile, didn't quite succeed. "You were amazing, yet again."

Tre grinned at me, but I could see the residual fear still bubbling behind his eyes. "I just, I couldn't let nothin' happen to you, Shea. Not at the hands of that—that—bastard."

"You protected me," I said, feeling the adrenaline kick in now, after the fact, as boiling heat in my belly, a trembling anticipation in my thighs.

I don't know if Tre saw something in my eyes, or if he felt it himself, but his eyes darkened with desire, his nostrils flaring. His hand snaked across the space between us to touch the bare skin of my leg, just below the hem of my shorts. The boy's boxer's he'd thrown at me were loose, riding low on my hips and loose around my legs. They were something I usually slept in, rather than wore out in public, but now I was suddenly glad for their looseness.

His fingers slipped higher, moving from the solid muscle of my quad inward to the soft silk of my inner thigh. I slid down in the leather seat until the lap belt creased the light padding over my ribs beneath my breasts. My knees spread apart to give him access. He didn't rush, though, and I knew I'd taught him well. He drew out the moment of contact, brushing close and drawing away, keeping his eyes on the road and letting his fingers explore by touch.

One finger brushed the line between my nether lips, releasing a spurt of wetness from within me. The same finger slid across my opening, searching upward for the hard button of my clit. I gasped when he found it, circled it once, and then slid down between my labia to penetrate inward, seeking the warmth and wet of my pussy.

My eyes pressed closed, bright mid-afternoon sun flickering on my eyelids as we passed beneath trees. The engine hummed, wind roared around the open top of the convertible luxury car, and Tre's fingers explored farther in, finding the rough skin of my G-spot and rubbed it, eliciting another gasp from me.

Back out and to my clit, swirling around it in circles. I was drenched, ready for a rhythm, wanting the burst of climax. I wanted him to pull the car over and take me in the passenger seat.

I forced my eyes open and examined our surroundings. We were surrounded by lush, rural Mississippi beauty, the two-lane road empty in front of us and behind us. I noticed a dirt track leading off into the woods to our right. I pointed at it, meeting Tre's eyes. He grinned widely and pulled off the highway, following the track through the woods and into the forest depths. The expensive Aston Martin wasn't meant for dirt roads, bumping on ruts and pits in the neglected packed dirt. The track broke off again, and Tre followed the new off-branching, going barely ten miles per hour to preserve the suspension, and our bodies, from the rough jouncing ride.

Suddenly, within less than a mile from the highway, we were in a whole different world. The powerful engine purred quietly, barely breaking the silence of the forest. After another few hundred feet, Tre stopped the car and shut off the engine. It ticked and popped as it cooled, and after a moment or two the birds began chattering once more.

Tre's fingers had been busy while he drove away from the main highway, diving in and pulling out, circling my aching clit, teasing me with arrhythmic touches. Now, with the car stopped and his attention focused on me, he began to swirl around the nexus of nerves in narrowing circles. My hips began to buck and writhe in time with his fingers, and now fire began to spread in billowing waves from deep in my core throughout my body. The forest echoed with the whimpered gasps of pleasure ripping from my lips.

I came with a shriek, curling inward and then arching my back.

I went limp for a moment, and Tre smiled in satisfaction, watching me regain my strength. I sat up when the trembling in my thighs and belly had subsided to a manageable quaking.

I grinned at him, and then unbuckled, popped open the car door and slid out to circle around to the front. I watched Tre over my shoulder through the windshield as I lay on my back on the warm hood. One arm stretched over my head, I curled a finger at Tre, beckoning him. The seatbelt slid away from his chest and he got out of the car. While he circled the car to stand in front of me, I unhooked my bra and slid my arms out of the straps, leaving my shirt on, and then tossed the bra over the top of the windshield into the front seat.

Tre's hard body slipped between the V of my thighs to press against me, and his hands slid up my belly, pushing my shirt up as they went. The hard bulge of his cock strained the zipper of his jeans. I lifted my arms, and Tre tugged the cotton past the gravity-flattened mounds of my breasts, over my head, and left it on the hood next to me. His lips lowered to my skin between my breasts, then traced a line of light, tongue-fluttering kisses across to one taut nipple.

I unbuttoned his jeans, unzipped them, pushed them down past his hips, and then reached into his boxers for the hard heat of his cock. He jerked in my hands and grew thicker at my touch. His hair was in my face, and I inhaled deeply, smelling shampoo. I rubbed my thumb over the crown of his cock, drawing the pre-come from its tip, then smeared the viscous liquid down over his length with my palms.

Tre nibbled a nipple and I gasped sharply. He tugged my shorts and the panties down together, my hips lifting of their own accord, and then I was bare on the hot red metal of the car hood. Tre's mouth was on my breast, his cock in my hands, birds twittering and chattering in the branches above us, a light breeze weaving through the branches.

I felt myself drawn down the hood toward Tre, and I lifted my legs to rest them on his shoulders. His lips met mine in the instant of his shaft piercing into me, swallowing my moan. He thrust slowly, gliding in to bump hips and drawing out so only the tip remained within me. He paused there, his eyes burning into mine between the frame of my legs. He stroked in again, stretching my legs into my chest as he leaned forward, filling me to bursting, achingly saturated with his length and width.

He curled his fingers around my ankles next to his ears, lips parted in an outbreath, eyes heavy-lidded as he pulsed into my tight folds. I'd just come, but I felt the quivering begin in my belly, felt Tre's rhythm increasing and heard his breathing grow ragged.

Then he slowed and paused.

"What is it?" I asked.

He seemed shy, like he wanted to ask something, but was afraid to.

I fluttered my hips as I said, "If you want to do something, do it. I trust you."

Tre lowered my legs from his shoulders and set me on my feet, his cock slipping out of me in the process. I blinked and gasped at the sudden absence, especially nearing climax as I had been.

When I was standing, he grabbed my hips and turned me in place. I knew what he wanted by then, but I played dumb. I turned my head, flashing him a coy smile, waiting. He kissed me over my shoulder, then put his palm between my shoulder blades and ever so gently pushed me forward so I was bent over the car. I spread my feet apart and rested my weight on my forearms, still watching him over my shoulder, my hair falling in a cascade onto the hood.

The last time we'd done this, I'd taken his cock in my hand and guided him into me. This time, I waited for him.

He caressed my spine from the nape of my neck down to my tailbone, cupped one half-globe cheek of my ass in his large hand, then ran his other hand from my breast along the curve of my side to my hip, gripping the other cheek. The satin-wrapped iron of his cock was pressed in the crease of my ass, and he used his hands to spread my cheeks apart, clutching his cock in one hand now and tracing down the split line to my essence-slick slit, immersing himself into my pussy again. I gasped as he thrust into me, once, hard, and then pulled out slowly and softly.

His hands gripped my hips and pulled me backward onto him, into his hips; I shrieked as he plunged deep enough to grind his hips against the muscle of my ass, lifting up on his toes and driving deeper. Climax rose up within me like a surging floodtide, washing through me. He pulled back, adjusted his grip on my hipbones, his wide hands spanning my waist, and then thrust in, fully and slowly. When he was inside me to the hilt, he continued to thrust, rising up on his toes, his entire torso, lifting my ass higher with his hands, driving so deep I couldn't even gasp. I was fully supported by only his cock and his hands, my mouth quivering wide in a silent scream.

He pulled out, holding me aloft for a heartbeat, and then let me go so I fell onto his cock. He slammed into me with an upthrust, and I came with a blinding burst of light behind my eyes, a convulsive clenching of my muscles around his cock. He growled deep in his chest, coming at the same moment as me, gushing hot seed into me, thrusting hard and fast, coming with each plunge, not giving me time to fall back down before pushing back in.

Just when I thought I couldn't come any more, any harder, Tre snaked his hands between my belly and the car hood and down to my pussy, his fingers finding my clit and circling it gently as he continued to drive into me, more softly now. Aftershocks turned into a third orgasm, this even more violent than the last, my scream of raw ecstasy sending birds winging up into the sky.

Tre scooped me up with one arm under my legs and the other under my shoulders. He set me directly into the bucket seat of the car. I slumped back against the leather, panting and limp, sated into immobility.

Tre gathered our clothes and slid into the driver's seat, slumping back as I had.

"God...damn, Tre," I said, breathless still, "just... damn."

He reached over and took my hand, kissed the back of it. That action had my heart clenching.

"It wasn't...too hard was it?" he asked. "I'm always worried I'll hurt you doing it like that, but I just can't help myself, once I get going."

"Tre, do you trust me?" I asked.

He wrinkled his brow. "Yeah, but—"

"Then trust me." I mirrored his action from a moment before, kissing the back of his hand. "Did it sound like you were hurting me? Or did it sound like the best sex I've ever had?"

A hesitant grin curled one side of Tre's mouth, and I couldn't help but kiss the corner as it lifted.

"It sounded like the best sex you've ever had," Tre said.

"Damn straight it was," I said. "Although I can think of a couple other times with you that might rival it for the actual 'best ever' slot."

Tre slid his jeans on and pulled his T-shirt over his head, and I began dressing as well.

"I guess I just worry I'm gonna like, totally lose it sometime and really hurt you," Tre said as he started the car and took us back out onto the highway.

I sighed in exasperation. "Tre, let it go. Seriously. You're not going to hurt me. I'm not some delicate little flower that's going to bruise at the slightest touch. I like it rough. Not all the time, of course. Sometimes I like it sweet and gentle. So, for the love of God, quit apologizing and acting like you're some...ravaging brute, or something."

Tre laughed. "Okay, jeez, I get it." He grinned at me. "I could be a ravaging brute, though, if that's the kind of thing you're into."

I made a face of mock fear and pretended to huddle against the car door. "No, Mister Ravaging Brute, don't ravage me! I'm afraid of your monster cock!"

"You'd better be afraid! You've unleashed the beast, baby, and you're about to be ravaged!"

I cackled. "But you just did! Can't an innocent damsel get a break from all this ravaging?"

"No," Tre said, stabbing the air with his finger, "no breaks for you. All ravaging, all the time!"

"All the time?" I pretended to swoon. "I don't even get to sleep?"

"Nope. I'll ravage you in your sleep too. I'll even ravage you in the bathroom."

"Well, you've already done that, at least once," I said, with a lecherous smile.

"Hmmm," Tre put his finger to his chin, "So, I've ravaged you in the bathroom, in a bed, bent over a bed, on a couch, in a car—or, well, sort of—and on a car... I'm not sure there's anywhere left."

"Well," I said, "I can think of a few places."

"Oh yeah? Like where?"

"An elevator," I said. "Or a changing room, or on a boat, on an airplane, in the water...ummm...where else can you have sex?"

"You mean where can you that you shouldn't?"

I lifted an eyebrow at him. "Well, kind of, I suppose. I can't see a problem with having sex in public places, as long as you don't get caught. I'd imagine it would be kind of a rush, now that I think of it."

Tre made a face that told me what he was going to ask next. "Have you ever done it in those places?"

"Haven't we already had this conversation too?" I asked. "But, if you must know, no, I haven't. Not in any of those places. Actually, just now with you on the hood of the car was the first time I've ever even done it outside."

"Wanna try?" Tre asked.

"Try what?"

"All those places." He glanced at me, and I realized he wasn't kidding.

I stared at him. "Are you serious?"

He nodded. "Totally serious. It was for real hot doing it with you on the car, outside."

"You want to have sex with me in a public elevator? And you wouldn't be completely and totally horrified if someone walked in on us?"

He shrugged. "It would be embarrassing, sure, but like you said, it seems like it would be a rush."

"You're serious?"

"Why not?"

I shook my head. "I just didn't think you'd...I don't know. I guess I thought you'd be more conservative, for some reason. "

"Well, I guess you really did unlock something inside me," he said, putting his hand on my knee, his voice more serious now. "I mean, I just can't get enough of you. Even when I just had you, I want you again."

"Right now?"

"All the time," Tre said.

I put my hand on his leg and slid it upward, touching the zipper of his jeans. "It doesn't seem like you want me right now," I said.

"Well, keep on touching me. You'll see," Tre said, smirking.

I opened his pants and revealed his semi-erect cock, watching him through lowered lashes as I traced light lines on his firming flesh with my fingertips. I used only my fingers on him at first, sliding and twisting, rubbing in circles around the crown, tickling the fine hairs on his tightening sack, stroking the muscle just behind his balls and spreading the leaking clear fluid of his pre-come. He was fully erect again in no time. I unbuckled and leaned over him, touched my tongue to him.

He smelled and tasted of our combined essences, a strong musky flavor that was totally different from his usual clean male taste of salt and skin and man. It wasn't unpleasant, only different.

I wanted to do this differently than usual. Instead of taking him into my mouth, I added my own saliva to the juices smeared on his length, caressing him in a smooth, circular, rolling motion with my hands. When he began to roll his hips in time with my pumping, I paused with one hand to cup and squeeze and massage his engorged head with my palm. I licked the very tip of his cock with my tongue, kissing the side of it, all the while stroking his base with a fist, bringing his hips to a rocking rhythm again.

I ceased moving my hand once his motion started to become desperate, working his tip solely with my tongue, sliding it around the groove under the head, taking only the first inch into my mouth and sucking gently. I glanced up at him as I took him sideways into my mouth so his cock bulged out my cheek; his fists gripped the steering wheel so hard his knuckles were white.

I felt the tires buzz on the rumble strips at the road edge. "Eyes on the road, Tre," I said.

"Can't help it," Tre said through gritted teeth. "Watchin' you put my cock in your mouth is hot."

"Then pull over," I said, moving my hand on his length. "Wouldn't want to get in a wreck. That'd put a damper on our plans to have sex in public."

He pulled the car to a stop on the side of the road, watching me as I bobbed my lips around his first inch of hard, throbbing flesh. "Does that mean we're doing the sex-in-public list?"

"Mmmm-hmmmm," I hummed my affirmative response, and Tre's eyes fluttered at the vibrations.

An idea struck me, and I had to stifle my grin of anticipation. I had a feeling he'd be a little...surprised by what I was about to do, and I didn't want to give away my plan.

I continued to work his base with one hand and his pulsating head with my mouth. My other hand cupped his balls, massaged them, and then slid down farther to his taint, pressing in circles. He moaned and rocked his hips, and this time I didn't pause, but I did slow down my ministrations. I didn't want him to come, not yet.

My middle finger slid from his taint inward, and now Tre's eyes flicked to me in surprise and not a little consternation. "What—what're you doin', Shea?"

I smiled and licked his cock from base to tip, stretching him away from his body and stroking him with my fist, moving my finger closer and closer to my goal. Tre's eyes widened and his body went still as I found the tight hard knot of muscle and pressed, lightly at first. His eyes were locked on mine, his nostrils flaring and his mouth pressed in a thin, flat line.

"Trust me?" I left my finger in place, but didn't press inward, yet.

"I trust you all right," Tre said, "But—"

"But what?" I slowed my strokes on his cock as he began to near climax.

He hissed in frustration. "I don't know. I guess I never thought—"

I sped up incrementally and applied a tiny bit of pressure with my finger. "You did it to me, and I enjoyed it. A lot."

A little more pressure, and my fist moved faster. Tre closed his eyes and let his hips roll, driving his cock into my mouth. He wasn't objecting anymore, so I pushed in farther, slowly and carefully. His mouth split in a gasping 'O', and his body curled in even as his hips rocked faster. He was close, now. I let him thrust his length into my mouth, caressing his base in blurring rhythm, pulsing my middle finger deeper by subtle increments up to the first knuckle.

Tre's forehead was resting against the steering wheel between his clenched fists, fluttering his hips frantically, gasping, "Oh god, oh god, oh god."

I bobbed my head, taking him deep and then almost out, pausing with the tip between my lips to suck until my cheeks hollowed. Tre's teeth clenched and ground together audibly, and then he spasmed, arching backward without warning. I moved with him, sucking his head furiously and moving my fist along his length as fast as my hand would go, pulsing my finger back and forth. His entire body was rigid in the driver's seat, his face thrown back to the sky, his breath stuttering.

And then he came. Oh, my lord. He came so hard his seed shot down my throat before I had a chance to swallow, and then again. I kept sucking, kept sliding my hand on him, and he kept coming until I lost count of how many times he spurted thick, salty heat into my throat.

At long last his body went limp. At that moment, I heard the unmistakable and heart-stopping *whoop-whoop* of a police cruiser's siren behind us. I swore, and zipped and buttoned Tre back up as hurriedly as I could, then dug my cell phone out of my purse without sitting up. I waited until I heard the clip of the officer's boots. Before I sat up, I wiped my face clean on my sleeve.

Tre was limp, sweating, and panting. He turned his head on the headrest to regard the jowly, overweight officer. I sat up, clutching my cell phone.

"What exactly is going on here?" the officer demanded, his voice gruff and low.

"I dropped my cell phone," I answered. "It slid beneath his seat so far we had to stop to get it." I held up my phone.

The officer eyed Tre, who was slowly regaining composure. "Then what's wrong with him?"

"He's been a bit under the weather recently," I said. "Bit of a stomach ache, low fever. It's been coming and going, you know how it is. He'll be fine for a bit, and then it hits him again."

The officer didn't look like he believed me, but he seemed to realize he didn't have much choice. "Hmm. Well, move along. If the boy ain't feelin' good, you best get him home. Behind the wheel of a car ain't the place for him if he's sick. 'Specially one this expensive."

The officer's radio crackled at that moment, and he gave us both one last resentful, disbelieving glare before going back to his car. Tre's hand clamped around mine.

"Go, Tre," I said. "Drive. Slowly."

Tre nodded, once, a jerk of his head, and then pulled the car into gear. He slipped out into the lane and added speed slowly until the cruiser was out of sight.

"Holy shit," Tre breathed, and then laughed, an edge of hysteria to his voice.

"Holy shit is right," I said. "That was a close one."

He glanced at me, grinning. "Yeah it was. I thought he was gonna arrest us for sure."

I squirmed my hand out of his and touched his zipper. "And what'd you think about what I did?"

Tre shook his head. "I didn't know it was possible to come that hard. I mean, I thought I was going to actually explode right in half." He shifted in his seat. "I wasn't sure at first, about...where you put your finger. I'm still not sure how I feel about it, in some ways, but—"

"You liked the end result, though, right?"

He shook his head again. "It was unbelievable."

I happened to glance in the side mirror, and saw red and blue lights flashing far behind us. "I think you'd best gun it, Tre. And find a side road to pull off."

He didn't ask questions. He saw it, too. The engine roared and the vehicle bolted forward. We were already going nearly seventy, but when Tre floored it, the car jumped forward hard enough to squeal the tires and fishtail before he got it under control. The flashing lights fell away behind us, the empty road speeding past us in a green blur. A county road split across the highway ahead of us, and Tre slowed down, then jammed the brakes, spun the wheel, and gunned the engine again. The Aston Martin turned into a sideways slide, hit gravel, tires spitting, and rocketed forward, still on an angle. Tre righted the car again, slowing enough to let the back end straighten, and then powered the car forward. We heard a siren now. We were kicking up dust, and I knew we had to get off the dirt road.

I'd never run from a police car before, and I knew Tre hadn't either. My heart was pounding in my chest.

"We've gotta get off the dirt, Tre," I said. "It's leading him straight to us."

Tre just nodded. After half a mile or so, we came across a parallel highway and Tre pulled onto it, turning north, rather than back south. The engine roared and I watched the speedometer hit one hundred within seconds. Another county road dissected the highway and Tre turned onto it, eastward now. I twisted in my seat, scanning for the lights of the pursuing cruiser. I didn't see it, but kept watching anyway.

Tre wound his way from county road to highway in a maze of random turns, driving at reckless speeds. Eventually I knew we'd lost our pursuit. I pointed to a turn-off on the county road we were travelling, and Tre pulled over.

"We're clear," I said, flopping back in the seat.

Tre unclenched his hands from the wheel and fell back as well, scrubbing his face.

"Holy shit," he breathed.

"Holy shit is right," I said, then laughed. "Déjà vu."

We both cracked up in uncontrollable then, flushed with the hysteria of post-adrenaline rush.

"Does this mean we're fugitives, now?" Tre asked.

I couldn't tell if he was panicked or not.

"Possibly," I said. "I find it hard to believe Dan would call the cops, since he's not exactly always operated on the legal side of things, but when it comes to this car, anything's possible."

"I know this is an expensive car," Tre said, "but exactly how expensive?"

I laughed. "Tre, this car is worth almost half a million dollars. Three hundred thousand, easily."

"Fuck," Tre said. "That's a lot of money."

"It's more than most people make in two or three years. Especially down here." I glanced at Tre. "I don't think you understand how bad it will have pissed Dan off to know we took his car. This thing is his one true love. If he catches us, he'll kill us, now."

"And you said he could find us, wherever we went?"

I nodded. "Pretty much. I might be able to work out a deal with him, though."

"What kind of deal?"

"I'm pretty sure he'd do anything to get his car back intact. I'll contact Dan when we get to the coast. Tell him we have his car and we'll tell him where it is if he swears to leave us alone."

"Think it'll work?" Tre put the car back into drive and found the nearest highway.

I shrugged. "It's worth a try. It'll buy us time to get away, at least. There's no guarantee he'll keep his word once he has it back, though."

Tre blew out a long breath between his teeth. "What'd we do, Shea?"

I laughed. "Made an enemy?"

"I guess we did." He scrubbed his face with his palm. "So now what? Where do we go?"

I shook my head. "I'm not sure. I was thinking south, to the Gulf? Or the Caribbean? The money I stole from Dan is an account in the Bahamas. We could go there, get some cash and figure something out."

"You mean like really go all fugitive? Get fake identities and all that?"

I laughed. "Well, I hadn't thought of that, but sure. It's not a bad idea, actually. I wouldn't know the first thing about where to start, but we could figure it out together."

"Well that's it, then, I guess." Tre slammed his hand into the steering wheel.

I took one of his hands in mine. "You know there's no going back from this, Tre."

He just laughed. "Shea, there was no going back for me a long time ago. I was done for the moment I followed you up the hill behind my dad's church."

"Done for how?" I asked.

The silence was sudden, tense, and thick.

"Just done for. That's all. I couldn't go back to the way I was. 'Specially after you let me in your house." He glanced at me; he was evading, and I let him. "You was wearing this little sundress. I think you was the sexiest thing I ever seen, right then. 'Course, I ain't seen you naked, then."

I smiled. "Your accent is back." I rubbed my thumb on his knuckles. "You know what that means?"

"Nuh-uh," he said. "I mean, no."

"It means you're not answering my question."

He shifted in the seat and looked in the rearview mirror rather than at me. "I thought we wasn't—weren't, I mean—putting things in boxes."

"Things have changed a bit since I said that." I threaded my fingers into his. "I don't just mean our circumstances."

"Then what do you mean?"

I shook my head. "Nope. You first."

"God, Shea. You're killing me, here." He lifted our joined hands and scratched the side of his nose with a thumbnail, then kissed the back of my hand. "You really wanna have this talk now?"

"Can you think of a better time? Are you scared?"

He nodded. "A little, yeah. I don't know what's happening, what we're going to do. We're kind of stuck together now. And no, I guess now's as good a time as any."

"Is that a bad thing? Being stuck with me?"

Tre furrowed his brow. "'Course not. There ain't—isn't—anyone I'd rather be stuck with. Not in the whole world."

My heart skipped a beat. "But you don't know that many people."

"Don't need to. Just need to know you."

"And you don't mind that I'm an old lady?" I grinned to make it a joke, but he saw past it.

"Not if you don't mind that I'm a snot-nosed kid."

"Seriously, though. Does the age difference bother you?" I asked.

It was a question that had bothered me for a while but had never mustered the courage to ask.

He shrugged. "Not really. I mean, there's differences, I guess, sure. But they don't usually bother me. I don't like thinking about you with anyone else, but I know you have, and that's a part of who you are. I know there's gotta be times when I seem young to you. I know I grew up under a rock, and there's a lot I don't know about."

"Yeah, but you're good at what matters."

"Ravaging you?" He grinned.

I slapped his shoulder. "Be serious for a second," I laughed. "Yes, that too. But I meant other things. You may have grown up under a very small rock, but you know how to take care of me. You protect me. I feel safe with you. You may not be wise in the ways of the world, but you're there for me when I need you."

"How could I not be?" Tre asked. "You're amazing. I still don't know what you see in me, but if you want to be with me, I ain't gonna argue."

I stared out the window. This was turning intense. "I see you," I said, after a long silence. "You're not just a sheltered preacher's son. You're so much more than that."

His answer was quiet. "I am now, at least."

"You always have been, Tre."

We drove south in silence after that, fingers twined.

Seven

The Gulfport-Biloxi International Airport was hot, humid, and crowded. Tre had parked Dan's Aston Martin in the farthest corner of the bottom level of a long-term parking structure. The top was up, the doors locked. We took the key with us and locked it in a storage locker. My plan was to fly to Nassau and contact Dan there. I'd sent the key for the storage locker, which in turn had the key to Dan's car, by mail to Dan's casino in Atlantic City.

It wasn't a great plan, and I could see a lot of flaws in it, but it was the best I could come up with at the last minute.

We paid cash for two first class tickets to Nassau. The first class lounge was an amazing place, to a backwater country kid like Tre. We didn't dare entirely relax, yet, though, so we didn't drink. I'd feel safer once we got to Nassau.

The plane boarded, and we took our seats. It was crowded flight, every seat filled. Once we were airborne, Tre looked at me, and then the small bathroom, and then back at me. He wiggled his eyebrows. I looked around me at the packed seats, all the people. I felt a rush of excitement at the thought of sneaking into the bathroom with Tre. I'd never done anything like that before. For all my life experiences, I'd never done anything risky or potentially embarrassing. I'd run away with a perfect stranger, but that was different. I'd been suffocating in Savannah. Sex with Tre was always great, and I could imagine the thrill of doing it in a public bathroom.

The "fasten seat belts" light was off, so I stood up and moved past Tre to the aisle.

As I passed him, I leaned forward and whispered in his ear, "Wait a few minutes, then come in."

We'd both changed clothes in the airport, and I was wearing a calf-length skirt with a sleeveless blouse. I made my way to the bathroom, closed the door behind me, but didn't lock it. I slipped my panties off and balled them in my fist, then waited for Tre.

Was I really going to do this? In the bathroom of an airliner? Oh, my lord, yes. I most assuredly was. I felt a wet heat spreading between my thighs, damp desire. I lifted the hem of my skirt up and pressed my finger to my clit, and a lightning bolt struck. I pictured Tre, naked and eyes blazing, defending me. My circling finger sped up, and I had to lean back against the wall for support, my knees buckling from pleasure.

I was near climax when I heard the door latch moving and dropped my skirt, in case it wasn't Tre. It was, and his eyes were dark with desire. He locked the door behind him, and I wasted no time getting his shorts down around his ankles and his already-hard cock in my fist.

I turned him to sit on the toilet, hiked my skirt around my hips and lowered myself onto him, facing away. He speared into me, and I had to bite my lip to keep from crying out as he slid deep inside me.

"God, you're so wet," he breathed in my ear.

I leaned back as far as I could, nipped his earlobe as he thrust into me, swiftly and silently. "I was touching myself, thinking of you," I said.

He grunted in reply, kissing my neck. His fingers slid up my belly, underneath my blouse and tugged the cup of my bra down, accessing my nipple. His other hand skimmed down and touched my clit. I turned my face into his, pressing my lips against his rough-stubbled cheek.

His thrusts were slow and powerful, and I could feel how close he was, already, thick and throbbing within me. His finger sliced in fiery circles around my aching clit, driving me to silent, searing orgasm. He gritted his teeth together so hard I could hear them creaking in his jaw; his fingers pincered around my nipple as he came, and I gasped out loud, and Tre's hand slid from my pussy to my mouth, silencing me as I whimpered. His seed flooded my walls and his fingers rolled my nipple, his hand across my mouth smelling of my musk, mingling with the dank scent of the airliner bathroom.

When he finally stopped his frantic plunging into me, I stood up. He reached for the toilet paper as I did, and he cleaned me with tenderness that took my breath away. As odd and unappealing as it seemed, there in the tiny, smelly bathroom of a passenger jet was when I realized the truth of my feelings for Tre. He cleaned me after our lovemaking, carefully and thoroughly, and something about that intimate action broke down the last of my resistance to him.

I gazed down at him, letting my emotion show through my eyes. He saw it, and opened his mouth to speak, but I silenced him with a kiss.

"Not now, Tre," I whispered. "Wait, and then come out."

I still had my panties stuffed in one fist. I handed them to Tre with a grin, and then adjusted my skirt, smoothed my ruffled hair, and left the bathroom. I found my seat and pretended to be absorbed in the celebrity gossip magazine I'd brought with me. A minute or two later, Tre resumed his seat by the aisle. I'm pretty sure we earned a few knowing smirks and snickers, but none of the flight attendants approached us.

When we were comfortable and it seemed no one was going to throw us out of the plane mid-flight, Tre turned to me and leveled a look that told me he wanted to talk.

"In the bathroom," he began, "you seemed—"

"Yes, things are changing, for me," I cut in. "When we first started out, I wasn't sure what it was between us. Honestly, at first, I just wanted you. You're so hot, so different from anything I've ever known. You're sweet and genuine and caring. You seem to like me for me, not just for sex."

"Of course I like you for more than sex," Tre said. "Is there any other way?"

I laughed, honestly amused at his naïveté. "Tre, in a situation like ours—I mean aside from the whole car-stealing business and whatever—most guys would be just in it for the sex. As soon as that stopped being fun, or I stopped being interesting or taking care of them, they'd be gone."

Tre sat back, thinking. "Do you feel like you're taking care of me?"

That wasn't the question I'd expected. "I don't know. I mean, yeah, kind of. Financially, at least."

Tre made a face. "I don't like that. I want us to be... partners, or equals. You shouldn't be taking care of me. I know you've got money, but I can work. I can make money."

"I know. But that's not really important right now, is it?"

He shook his head. "No, guess you're right. We can figure that out once we sort out—"

"Everything else. Like, what are we? Where are we going? What's our long-term plan?"

"So we're ready for boxes, then?" Tre asked.

I bobbled my head side to side. "Boxes? I don't like boxes. But, I like being with you. I know that much. I really, really like having sex with you. I feel safe and comfortable with you. And, I promise, I do believe you're capable of providing. We may not need it, since I'm pretty set, but it's nice to have, you know?"

"Yeah. It's stolen, though, and I'll be honest, a part of me is uncomfortable with that. I haven't had much choice since leaving Yazoo, obviously, but if we go somewhere, I'll find a job. I can do anything." He twisted in his seat to face me. "So, are we together, then?"

I laughed. "Yes, we are. I mean, assuming you want to be?"

"Of course I do," Tre said. "I can't picture anyone else."

"Well, you haven't been with anyone else, have you?"

"No, and I don't want to be with anyone else." Tre shrugged, dismissing the idea.

Silence for a while, then I asked, "So, then, where are we going from Nassau?"

Tre laughed. "Well hell, I don't know. I've never left Mississippi." He stared out the window, then turned back to me. "I guess we could just take it one day at a time. See where we end up, where we like to be, and stay there."

It was a simplistic way of putting it, I thought. But then, why couldn't it be simple? Just find somewhere we like to be, and stay there?

It suddenly sounded like a wonderful idea.

We hired a private flight from Nassau to St. John's. We'd moved my account, taken some cash, and left Nassau within twenty-four hours. It was too local, too familiar, too easy to find. I wanted to be somewhere obscure.

We sat in the back of the twin-engine float plane, hand in hand, watching the ocean ripple beneath us. The pilot was a taciturn, bearded, older man who'd taken our cash and lifted off without a word, no names asked, no flight plan logged. We'd paid extra for that service.

He set down off shore, props still spinning. Tre offloaded our luggage into the waiting outboard motor skiff, and the plane was gone within seconds. The boat pilot nodded and smiled, but didn't speak.

A few minutes of bouncing on the pale blue waves and we were bumping against a dock, surrounded by a forest of bobbing masts. Once again Tre threw our luggage—two suitcases and two carry-on backpacks—to the dock and we left the boat, which backed out and puttered away.

St. John's. Tre and I glanced at each other, at the lush, tropical vegetation and dots of houses peeking from between the trees, and then back at each other. A taxi skidded to a stop next to us and a young man with curly black hair jumped out, grabbed our suitcases and threw them into the open trunk.

"Come, come. Hotel, this way," the young man said, waving to us.

Tre shrugged and climbed into the taxi, pulling me after him. The taxi ride was frightening. I'd been on rollercoasters less hair-raising. The driver dodged between trucks full of produce, other taxis, private vehicles, mopeds, and pedestrians, all at a breakneck pace, honking. I clutched Tre's hand and laughed, a little hysterical.

The taxi came to a screeching stop at a Sheraton. The driver jumped out, carried our luggage into the lobby without consulting us.

"Come, come. Best hotel. Luxury hotel. Stay. Enjoy Love City," he said, a bright smile showing rows of white, even teeth against his dark skin.

We paid him and went in, deciding to go with the flow.

"You know he probably gets a kickback from taking us here," I told Tre.

He shrugged. "I'm sure. But does it matter? Now we don't have to look for somewhere to stay right off the bat. We'll figure something out long term later. For now, let's just chill."

"Chill?" I grinned. "What kind of chilling?"

Tre licked his lips and leaned close to whisper his answer as we approached the concierge. "The kind where you don't have any clothes on."

I laughed. "Well, of course. Is there any other kind?"

"Nope."

We got a room on the twentieth floor, a single. We spent the day touring downtown St. John's, doing the tourist thing. We didn't go back to the hotel until well after midnight, footsore and happy.

The lobby was deserted, only a bored concierge on duty behind the desk. The elevator was equally deserted. Tre had my skirt up around my hips within seconds, his fingers brushing into me.

"Tre," I laughed, "you have to push a button for the elevator to move."

"I will," he muttered, lifting my shirt to take a nipple into his mouth.

"What if someone wants to take this elevator?" I asked.

"There's others."

He silenced any further questions by kissing me, one hand between my legs, stroking me gently, sending heat billowing through me. I hadn't been horny when we got on the elevator. I'd been looking forward to a hot shower and a soft bed, and Tre's arms around me as I slept.

I couldn't resist his tongue's sweep against my lips, his fingers delving into my soft folds, which grew wetter and readier with every passing moment. I couldn't resist his hand cupping my breast, his lean hips pressing me against the elevator wall. Most of all, I couldn't resist his urgency, the desperation with which he touched and kissed and held me. As if he'd starved his whole life for the attention I offered.

His desperation fueled my own, and I realized I was as in need of affection as he was. It was suddenly no longer just about his fingers in my pussy or his tongue in my mouth, or his hard cock in my hands as I felt myself lifted up and pinned against the wall. It was about him. It was about the reason he touched me, the delicate fury of his slow penetration into me. It was about the light in his eyes as he lifted me up and slid me down to bury his shaft inside me.

It was about his voice in my ear, whispering my name. "Shea, oh god, Shea."

It was my reply, torn from my lips: "How have I lived my entire life without you?"

He didn't answer, just lifted up on his toes as I lowered my hips, and whispered my name again.

Neither of us slowed or stopped when the elevator dinged and the door whooshed open. "Oh, shit.

Um, excuse me," came a shocked male voice. The doors closed and we were alone again.

Tre laughed into the skin of my neck, and then fell silent once more. I dragged my fingertips across his jaw, turned his face up to mine, kissed him, eyes open, tried once again to let what I was feeling show through.

He came with soft gasp, and I came with him, our lips touching in a stilled kiss.

After another moment of heaving breath and sparking, meeting eyes, Tre let me down and touched the button for our floor. It was a short ride and a shorter walk to our room. He swiped the card and shoved open the door.

His seed was running down my leg as he stripped me of my clothes. Naked himself, now, he scooped me in his arms and set me on the bed. I watched his tight ass move as he set the tub to filling with steaming water, then came back for me.

Neither of us had said a word since we'd entered the hotel.

He stretched out on the bed next to me, our skin pebbling in the cool air of the hotel, and ran his hands on my skin, touching me everywhere. He began at my face, brushing stray strands of hair from my cheek, kissed my nose and forehead and cheekbones, then my mouth and my neck. His fingers roved across my shoulders, down my arms, tangled with my hands and then back to my ribs, lifted the weight of my breasts and kissed underneath them, the mounded sides, and then the taut nipples, each in turn. His fingers drifted southward along my belly while his mouth remained at my breasts.

I felt his cock against the outside of my thigh, a soft lump between us. The water poured into the tub, the only sound in the room but for my soft sighs. I took his soft manhood in my hands and rolled in it my palm, turning on my side to watch it grow at my touch. It was gradual at first, just a twisting of the curled, limp flesh, veins straightening. Then there was subtle firming of the skin, a tightening of the sagging skin of his balls. I traced the length of him with a fingernail, and his cock jerked, grew perceptibly larger. It no longer hung down to lay against his thigh, but rather stood semi-erect, as if in anticipation.

His hand carved down the curve of my hip to my thigh, cupped my ass and continued its downward slide to my thigh, running along the outside. When he reached the extent of his arm's length, his hand drew upward once more, this time along the inside. My thighs trembled in delicious preparation of his soft, insistent, tender touch.

His fingers parted my thighs, traced the crease of my labia. I sighed in pleasure, and his cock went rigid in my hands. I caressed his length in a loose fist, barely brushing his veined flesh. His cock was a heated steel rod in my hands, swathed in softest silk, pulsing with blood, aching for my touch, bobbing with his breathing, tip glistening with dewdrops of pre-come.

And then I was airborne, lifted effortlessly in his brawny arms and carried to the tub, lowered gently into the steaming water. He turned off the faucet and climbed in behind me, sloshing water over the side. I lay with my back against his chest, his cock jammed between our bodies. I turned my face up to kiss his jaw, wrapped my arm behind me and pulled his head down to mine. Our lips met, bumped, touched, and then locked together. Heat diffused through us, from the water and from our bodies, from the steam in the air and the fires of desire in our bellies.

He slid his hands beneath my ass and lifted me up. I braced myself with feet and hands, still kissing him, and then reached down between us and guided the thick crown of his shaft to my entrance. He didn't thrust in immediately, but wrapped his hands beneath my thighs and held me aloft as he gently and slowly nestled himself inside me, a centimeter at a time, careful to not break the suction keeping the water out of me.

By the time he was buried to the hilt, his arms were trembling from supporting my weight. He drew his knees up and slid down in the tub so I was sitting on top of him, impaled by him. I leaned back and rested my head on his shoulder, cupped his face in my hands and whispered his name as our bodies rocked in slow, undulating rhythm, sending waves of bathwater rippling between us.

His lips crushed against mine again, stealing my breath in a searing kiss. Gentle hands brushed my shoulders and slid down my backbone, caressed both breasts and squeezed them, pinched the nipples and rolled them, causing my hips to buck in affirmation. I moaned into his mouth when one of his hands descended the slope of my belly and dipped without pause into my pussy. I used my feet against the far side of the tub as leverage to lift my hips and sink down on his hard, scorching shaft, moaning loudly now.

He continued to toy with my sensitive nipples and circle the hard nub of my clit as he thrust into me, gasping in tandem with me now. His heartbeat was a steady drum against my back, his voice an encouraging groan in my ear, his body both hard yet soft beneath me, driving into me in a way that filled me as never before, striking deep, deep within me.

As his body penetrated mine, I felt his heart and soul piercing me as well. As in the bathroom, and in the elevator, this sensate experience with Tre delved far beyond the pale of mere sexual contact. It was a turning point, of sorts. It had been coming for a long time, building in incremental degrees, and this was the apex.

Water sloshed around us, our moans of bliss morphed into cries of ecstasy, voices twined, bodies rocking in pulsating synchronicity, raw emotion coiling like serpents in the air, unspoken but all too real.

And then he changed everything.

He came, saying, "Goddamn, Shea. I love you so much."

The climax that burst through me was as much emotional as physical. I hadn't heard those words in so, so many years. They knifed into my heart as his essence washed through me, as his body merged with mine. I felt my inner muscles clamp down around him and my arms clenched around his neck, my lips locked on his and I came with a deep, wracking sob.

"Oh god, Tre. Oh god. Yes." I gripped his hair in my fist and craned my neck to peer into his eyes. "Say it again, Tre."

He thrust hard into me. "I love you, Shea." Another thrust, and my eyes closed involuntarily at the piercing pang of pleasure. "I love you."

I cried and laughed, rocked my body on his, and climaxed with every fiber of my being. My body curled down onto him, and I was helpless against the writhing bliss that rocketed through me, aftershock upon aftershock.

Our shudders subsided and I could breathe once more. I lay on him in the tub, still impaled by him. I opened my mouth to speak, but he kissed me quiet.

"Don't say it just to say it back," Tre told me. "Say it if and when you want to, because it's what you feel."

I nodded, and let myself go limp. We drowsed in the water until it went cool and then drained it, stood and turned on the shower to clean up. We toweled each other dry, trading kisses on random patches of revealed skin, and then cuddled together in the bed, the cool sheets warming quickly with our body heat.

I slept, long and deep, waking to a crack of morning light piercing between the gap in the heavy curtains. The air beyond the covers was cold, smelling of hotel air conditioner. Tre was on my left, his face lax in sleep, thick black hair sleep-mussed and drifting across his cheek and forehead. I swept it aside with my finger, and he nudged his face into my palm in his sleep, like a puppy seeking affection.

He stirred, rolling from his back to his side, seeking me with his hands. I let him pull me close, clutch me against him. He wedged one of his thighs between mine, his arm flung over my hip possessively. His cock was hard, poking into my belly, a hot length stabbing just beneath my ribs.

I lay awake, watching him sleep, feeling the last bricks in the wall around my heart crumble.

I loved him.

The realization didn't frighten me.

I wasn't aware at first of my hands drifting between us to curl around his cock. His eyes cracked open and a smile touched the corners of his lips. He didn't move or speak, just gazed at me through half-lidded eyes. I just held him at first.

Then I lifted my leg and hooked it over his hip and guided the tip of him to the damp heat of my entrance. I didn't slide him in, yet. His eyes opened farther, and his hand tightened on my hip.

"I love you, Tre." A shift of bodies, and he slipped in. It was the most natural feeling in the world, now, to feel him fill me. "God, I don't know how it happened, but I love you."

Tre chuckled, a low rumble in his chest. "It happened because we're meant for each other."

Silence, fire and motion and slow breaths in the cool air.

"You think we're meant to be together?" I asked, tangling my fingers in the soft curls at the back of his neck.

"Yep," he said, his hand on the small of my back, pushing me closer against him. "You're my home. Yazoo City was just the place I grew up. I don't care where we are, or where we go, or what we have or don't have. All's I need is you, Shea."

I melted. I was curled around him, filled by him, caressed and held and loved by him. Our motions were slow, unhurried, no longer desperate. Each pulse of his body into mine was a glide of his heart further into me, a slip of his soul tighter around mine, a tangling of his life more thoroughly with mine. We clawed at each other, lips touching faces and shoulders, teeth biting and nails digging, all in an attempt to draw more completely into the other.

I wanted to be inside him, to be not me, not us, but one single person all melded and braided from the twin skeins of self.

We moved thus together for what might have been an eternity. All I knew was the glint of morning light in his eyes, the soft strength of his hands. I was above him now, riding him, leaning back and devouring the sensation of his body in mine, under mine. And then I was beneath him, no sense of movement, just a flash of spinning room and his body sheltering me from the world, from time, from all things but him, him, all of him surrounding me, within me, beside me. I saw him, and I knew him, and I felt him, and I knew I could never, ever forget this moment of love for as long I'd live. His eyes burned into mine, his skin scorched mine where our bodies met, so hot I thought we might melt and meld together.

Orgasm is a physical sensation. It's the rush of chemicals in your brain, the clench and release of muscles and fluids and pleasure.

Climax is the peak of the sexual process, whereby orgasm is achieved. It's the infinitesimally brief instant of pleasure.

What happened with Tre and me in that hotel room was something else, something different. Is there an emotional orgasm? A heart-gasm? A soul-gasm? A self-gasm?

Complete and total contentment is so rare, so unattainable by most everyone, that to experience it is orgasmic. Complete and total happiness is equally as rare. True, pure physical ecstasy also is nearly impossible to find. All three at once?

I grew up believing in God the way most people believe in the power of a chair to hold their weight, the way they believe in gravity. Then I ran away with a charming casino magnate and learned the harsh realities of life, and stopped believing in God.

What I experienced with Tre was a reunion with God. I swear I saw a fragment of heaven in the moment of climax, when Tre and I were truly a single ephemeral being caught up in a swirl of light of purity and pleasure and perfection.

In the moment of stillness, with the afterglow shining on our skin, our eyes met, and words were whispered into the sweet silence.

"I love you."

I don't know who actually said them. I was thinking them, and I saw them glimmering in his eyes, and I heard them.

That's all that mattered.

Eight

A year later I was selling real estate and Tre owned a deep sea fishing charter boat. We lived in a modest two room villa on St. Croix, and we had a quiet life.

Well, some things were quiet. What I mean is, we never heard from Dan, or Tre's parents.

The day we bought Tre's boat was pretty memorable, and not so quiet. He'd worked for several months for a man who ran a deep sea fishing charter, and having fished frequently in Mississippi, Tre took to it naturally. He brought up the idea of owning his own boat one night when we were lying on a blanket on the beach below our house, sharing a bottle of wine and basking in the warmth of a balmy night.

I thought about it, and realized it made more sense for him to own his own boat than work for someone else, so I agreed. We went out the next day and looked at boats, which he'd obviously been researching for some time. He had his options narrowed down to three good-sized vessels, one of them already completely outfitted for a charter being sold by a man ready to retire from twenty years of deep sea fishing. He bought that one, a sleek, attractive ship named *The Sea Dancer*.

I think Tre had already come to an agreement with the seller, actually, since we were able to take possession immediately. I wrote a check, handed it to the man, who in turn handed Tre the keys and title, and simply walked away down the dock, whistling a merry tune.

Tre backed *The Sea Dancer* out of the slip and guided it skillfully out of the bustling sunset-lit bay. We headed out to open sea, Tre standing shirtless at the wheel, a Bulldogs baseball cap backwards on his head, cutoff shorts hanging low on his hips. I stood behind him, running my hands on his smooth chest, lips pressed to his shoulder, watching the muscles in his arms ripple gently as he guided the ship into the orange ball of the setting sun.

Once again I was struck by a heart-aching burst of pure happiness. I think people aren't meant to be truly happy all the time. It's simply too potent a feeling to tolerate in large quanties.

About half an hour out, Tre brought the boat to a stop and let it drift, low waves clapping against the sides of the boat and sending it rocking and swaying.

Tre led me down to the bow, sat me down, and returned to the cabin. He came back with a bottle of champagne in a bucket of ice, a vase of red roses, and a spread of food.

"This wasn't a sudden decision, was it?" I asked.

Tre shook his head, biting into a strawberry. "Nope. Been planning this for a while now. Old Ben, there, the guy we bought this boat from, he was one of the first fishermen I made friends with. When he said he was callin' it quits, I asked him to sell it to me. So, here we are. Only, I arranged all this before time, so we could have this little date."

I laughed and kissed him. "What if I'd not wanted you to be a fisherman forever?"

It was his turn to laugh. "But you don't mind, and I knew you wouldn't."

We ate in silence for a few minutes more, and then, when the sun had finally lowered beneath the horizon and all was golden light, Tre set aside the plates of food and turned to face me. We were both sitting cross legged on the bow, wind in our hair and waves chucking against the boat.

Tre reached into his pocket and pulled out a ring. My throat swelled up, thick and hot.

"I ain't much for makin' pretty speeches, Shea. You know that. I love you, more than anything. More than life itself." He took my hands in one of his, emotion in his eyes and in the sudden drawl of his words. "You and I have an amazing life together already. I don't need nothin' to change. But I'm an old fashioned kinda guy, I guess. Some things you just cain't get rid of, even if you move to the U.S. Virgin Islands. I want to be your husband."

He held up the ring. "Be my wife, Shea Harley?"

I choked. "Tre, I love you. So much, but—"

He interrupted me. "There's one thing I ain't told you. I set up a post office box over on St. Thomas, in a different name. Had a guy help me with it. Well, I also paid a lawyer I took fishin' a few months back to do some work for me." Tre trotted into the cabin and came back with a manila envelope and handed it to me.

I opened it. Signed and completed divorce papers. With Dan's signature. All it needed was mine. I stared at the papers, something I'd not dared to hope I'd ever see, my eyes wavering, burning. A pen appeared in my line of sight and I took it, glanced up at Tre, and then signed. He stuffed the papers back in the envelope and sealed it, took it back to the cabin. When he came back, my eyes were dry, but still burning with yet-unshed tears.

"So, let me ask again." He knelt on the bow of our boat, ring held out to me. "Marry me, Shea?"

I sniffed, struggled to hold back my tears, and failed. All I could do was nod, rising up on my knees to kiss him. He pulled away, slipped the ring on my finger, and then kissed my palm.

I was wearing an orange sarong, and Tre brushed it off my shoulder, let it fall to the deck around me. He unhooked my bra with unsteady fingers, focusing on one hook at a time. He stuck his tongue out as one hook refused to come free, and I was reminded of our first time together, back in Yazoo. He was so innocent, so young. He was only a year older, now, but almost a different person, in so many ways. Still the same, sweet, considerate Tre, but a man, confident and strong.

The hook eventually came loose and he set my bra aside, then hooked his thumbs in the elastic of my panties, drew them down and set them aside as well.

I had one question. "Tre?" He was busy kissing down from my shoulder to my breast, and didn't look up. "You still want to marry me, even I can't give you kids?"

He froze, looked at me, then nodded. "Of course. We can always adopt, if things come to that. I love you and want to be with you forever. That's all that counts, to me."

He kissed the tears as they fell, yet again. I let him dry my face with his thumbs, and then attacked him with a flurry of kisses, knocking him over onto his back. I kissed him with everything I had, stripping him of his shorts so he was naked beneath me. He slid into me, and oh, my lord, he felt so right inside me.

There had never been anyone else in my life, in that moment. Only Tre. Only his hands had ever smoothed over my skin, had ever drawn gasps of pleasure from me, as they did then, rolling my nipples in strong, gentle fingers. Only he had ever slid into me and pulled out in that sinuous, satisfying way. Only he had ever kissed me as if I was the light to his hungry darkness.

His love erased the past, so there was only future.

We made love until the sky turned charcoal with the approach of night. I spent many long minutes between sessions staring at the glint of evening light on the diamonds of my ring. He'd bought it with the money earned fishing. His money, not mine. That was important to him. And to me, even more, I realized.

We drank the champagne in between lovemaking, and when it was gone and we were sated, Tre turned on the lights and plied the waves back home.

We were married on the beach at sunset, three months after he asked me. There were only a few people there with us, a few fishing buddies of Tre's, a couple realtor friends of mine, and some village friends of both of ours. We didn't need a honeymoon, because we lived in paradise.

The burst of pure happiness? The one I said earlier people couldn't handle if they had it all the time?

I was wrong. You can be truly, purely happy. There are moments of strife, of course. Arguments over misspoken words, ill-thought decisions, the usual things that make up life. Happiness, I've discovered, is a choice, a habit. It's a mindset.

A strong, loving man who can give you half a dozen orgasms in one night definitely helps, though.

The End

About the Author

New York Times and USA Today bestselling author Jasinda Wilder is a Michigan native with a penchant for titillating tales about sexy men and strong women. When she's not writing, she's probably shopping, baking, or reading. She loves to travel, and some of her favorite vacations spots are Las Vegas, New York City, and Toledo, Ohio. You can often find Jasinda drinking sweet red wine with frozen berries.

To find out more about Jasinda and her other titles, visit her website: www.JasindaWilder.com.